𝕭irthright

Destiny Bound
Book One

Alexis Kennedy

Other Books by Alexis Kennedy

Bound Through Blood

Under the Blood Moon

Ravaged (Dial M for Murder Book 1)

Déjà vu (Dial M for Murder Book 2)

Cupid   (Dial M for Murder Book 3)

Two Faced

Scandalous

Angry House

Birthright

Indelible (Two Faced book 2)

https://alexiskennedy.net

"A writer's work is never done. A book can be done, and your edits can be done, but you'll always be writing as long as your characters are talking to you."

~Alexis Kennedy

one

1601 Transylvania

Red eyes peeked through the cover of trees. The prey stood not more than twenty yards away. He could see its breath swirling around its nostrils in the early-evening fog, and he could hear it snorting with its heavy breathing as it pawed the earth. Just another second or two and he'd make his move. He reared back on his haunches and broke through the brush at sixty-five miles per hour before pouncing. In a split second, he was on top of the writhing buck, biting into the animal's thick neck. He tore its throat out and began feasting on the warm salty flesh.

Not far from the smorgasbord, a couple embraced nature's guilty pleasure on the green grass. Their naked bodies entwined under the rolling fog, and soft moans of enjoyment echoed off the hillside. Their sounds of lovemaking drowned out the sounds of flesh being torn from bone only a matter of feet away from them.

Damian tossed the naked wench onto her back and buried his face between her taut quivering thighs. He would've preferred to take his time with the woman, but he felt starved. He licked, nibbled, and sucked on her thigh until she ran wet, writhed, and screamed for more. To answer her cries, he used his fingers to pleasure her while his other hand ran its nails down her wriggling leg. He could tell she was about to explode from her lust for him; he could feel it all around his finger, see it on her face, and hear it in her cries. His own need grew strong as well, and it wasn't just the one pulsing solid and steady between his muscular thighs. His thirst needed to be fed too. His razor-sharp fangs involuntarily elongated in response to the thought, and he ran his tongue over them. The woman's eyes were half closed from desire, so she didn't notice the change, which was good because he wasn't in the mood for a struggle. He rose to his knees and put her ankles on his massive shoulders. Then, as he forced himself inside her welcoming passage, he bit shallowly into her ankle and began to suckle her warm blood. Her life's force filled his greedy mouth, and its metallic scent his nostrils while her body thrashed in pleasure from his slow, steady strokes. As his energy was replenished, his tempo picked up, and he pulled away from her petite ankle to push her knees into her chest and pressed his body down on them. His girth filled her even deeper, and she squealed in delight. He grunted from his own enjoyment and then took a rosy bud into his hungry mouth. While suckling the taut peak, he pinned her wrists above her head, which seemed to arouse her more, and then he ran the tip of his tongue from her wet nipple up the mound and to her long luscious neck. He pressed gentle kisses around her pulse at first, playing with the rhythmic beat of her heart. Its steady throbbing called to him like a siren's song, and he answered by sinking his fangs into her delicate flesh. Luckily for her, his saliva contained a numbing agent, so she didn't feel much more than a playful nip. He fed his thirst with long pulls on her salty blood while his clawed hand kneaded her breast. The other still had her wrists pinned just in case she got feisty. She didn't struggle, though; she just moved metrically with each stroke he gave her and rode wave after wave of pleasure. He could feel her climaxes around his shaft squeezing and pulling him toward his own release. Then she stopped moving with him, and her chest ceased to rise and fall. As her last breath escaped her lips on a sigh, his culmination was upon him, and he filled her corpse with his heated lust.

Necrophilia? Maybe so. He chuckled softly to himself and rolled away from her lifeless body while licking the last droplet from his perfect lips. *Waste not, want not.*

He looked over at the woman with an ounce of pity and traced a nail down her bare chest. She was his second woman for the day—there had been breakfast too.

An exasperated sigh sounded from behind him followed by, "Are you done yet?" Logan, his brother, was always the impatient one, but that was probably the wolf in him.

"Yes, I'm done, and I don't interrupt *you* during dinner."

"Well, I don't play with my food the way you do"—he squinted his eyes in thought—"At least not always." A lopsided grin adorned his handsome face, and he tilted his head until his thick neck popped once on each side. "I'm bored. Can we go now?"

Damian looked around the tree line where they were. The question was, go where? There were three unknowns. They didn't know who'd killed their mother and abducted their father, they didn't know where to look for him, and they didn't know why war was waged, but they did know one thing for certain—someone would pay.

Now, he looked up at the sky and the setting sun, casting shades of pinks, oranges, and purples across the quickly darkening canvas, and grunted, "North."

"How far are we traveling tonight?"

Damian sighed deeply before answering his younger brother by all of two minutes. "We'll travel into Brasov and talk to the townsfolk in the sunup. Someone there has to have seen something." He led the way, and Logan followed right behind him.

"Do you think they'll talk to us? We aren't exactly known to them," Logan pointed out.

Damian slanted his eyes, grinned a toothy grin, and growled, "We'll make them talk."

Logan chuckled low in his throat and extended his claws, which he then swiped at the air. "Yeah, we will," he eagerly agreed.

If Lucian Dragovich, their father, was around, he'd order them to act dignified when in the presence of the townspeople because they were, in his eyes, still royalty even if the villagers no longer recognized the kingdom of Drago. When Lucian's father, King Titus, died, the throne died along with him. Lucian was too young to take it over, and his mother had already died years before. Mortality, unfortunately, was not a stranger to their breed. It is true, though, that the aging process remarkably slowed when maturity was reached around the age of twenty years.

They learned through research that vampires stopped aging altogether at about age thirty, but that didn't guarantee them an immortal existence either. This they knew from personal experience since much vampire blood was shed in the rescuing of Damian when he was two. To date, the twins were healthy, fully-fleshed twenty-one-year-olds with appetites for adventure, danger, sex, and revenge.

When the fraternal twins had been born, the chance for a rebirth of the kingdom had become possible since Lucian could, no doubt, stand strong with his two werewolf sons beside him at the throne. Hope had even sparked in the villages surrounding Drago until the vampires had kidnapped Damian, causing the embers to die down. When he had been safely rescued—but it had become evident that he had been turned into a vampire—the embers burned out altogether. Of the "immortals," vampires were the most feared—they were not at all trusted by the townspeople. One too many babe and maiden had been snatched away in the night by a blood-thirsty vampire.

While Damian was still accepted as Lucian's son, he was never looked upon or treated quite the same as Logan by the villagers. Then, when Lucian's boys had entered their teen years, the villagers side-stepped both of them when they were seen coming. However, it was for different reasons. Logan was mostly avoided because he was a shit-disturber and made trouble everywhere he went. Damian was simply feared. The werewolf-turned-vampire was the first of his kind, and no one knew what to expect from him. He didn't even know what to expect with the passing of time. But of course, at the moment, he had bigger things to worry about.

Logan must have read his mind because he suddenly blurted out, "What if they don't know?"

Damian drew a hand across his dark chiseled features in thought. "Someone knows."

"When do you want to take our rest?"

Damian could hear the fatigue in his brother's voice, and the truth was he was feeling it himself, so he replied, "Here. We'll stop here till sunup."

He removed his belted sword, tossed it to the ground, and then lay down on the soft earth. In their hurry, they'd grabbed their weapons and only a few wares to sustain themselves on their journey. In a sack, he'd thrown some dried salt pork and bread—blood wasn't the only food he consumed, although it was the most important and the tastiest. After his rescue, though, his father had made a promise to the nearby communities, when it became clear what Damian was. He'd promised that Damian would only feed upon the dying. He would be the Angel of Death and help them transition to the other side. And so it became an unwritten law. That is until Damian grew older and curious, and he started sneaking off to find lively prey on his own. That was also when he'd discovered the pleasures of women.

"Damian?" Logan's voice was hoarse with emotion, and it scared off some nearby wildlife.

"What is it?"

"I'm going to miss her," he answered softly this time, and Damian could hear him struggling with tears. A display of weakness, for any reason, was not acceptable behavior for a werewolf and especially not for the son of a king.

"Aye, me too," Damian grunted. "Get some sleep. We don't have long." Fortunately, they didn't need long. They only needed a couple of hours of rest each night to be able to maintain their stamina.

Loud snoring sounded from Logan's direction to announce his departure to the dream realm, and Damian smiled to himself thinking that maybe he'd see their mother there. Maybe they both would. He closed his eyes and drifted off too.

His dreams were fitful, though. He was taken back to the castle, to the moment when Logan and he knew something was wrong. It was too quiet, and then they spotted the blood. It was just a little at first, but the trail took them to bigger pools and finally to their mother's cold body.

Damian bolted upright hissing with his fangs showing, which caused Logan to jump to all fours, in pouncing position, with his fangs bared as well.

"Where?" Logan growled.

"Nowhere—it was just a bad dream," Damian admitted and felt foolish.

Logan stood up and popped his neck on both sides. "Well, since we are both awake anyway, I say we keep going. Brasov isn't too far from here."

Damian looked at the moon still hanging low in the sky. "Aye, let's keep going then." They grabbed their meager belongings and continued to tread northbound to the small village.

Two

The brothers reached the sleepy village of Brasov just as the sun peeked over the horizon.

"What's the plan?" Logan asked with an urgency in his voice. He was always ready for action, no matter where they were.

"We let them stir before we make our approach," Damian ordered. They weren't likely to receive a warm welcome, so it was best to give the villagers a chance to fully open their eyes before pressing them for answers.

Logan, who was anxiously pacing, took a deep whiff of the air. "I'm hungry," he growled. He looked to his left and peered at the row of huts neatly lined up, and before Damian could protest, he bolted toward a small gathering of chickens one hundred feet away and helped himself to a warm meal.

Damian was hungry too, but he couldn't seek out what he wanted, so instead, he reached into the knapsack he carried and tore off a piece of the salt pork. The taste meant nothing to him. It brought him no satisfaction to dine on dead food.

A scream pierced the morning air, causing a flock of crows in the nearby tree to beat their wings fiercely as they tried to get away and Damian's head to snap in his brother's direction. This wasn't how he wanted to announce their presence. What he saw made him chuckle to himself before he trotted to his brother's side. A female child was holding a pitchfork aimed at Logan.

"Put her down," she shrieked at Logan, who looked quite surprised. He glanced down at the struggling hen he held and then back to the child who jabbed the pitchfork in his direction. Then he looked at Damian, who gave one nod.

Frowning like a berated child, he snarled, "Fine," before tossing the fowl aside. The happy bird scampered away clucking loudly.

"Alina, what's wrong?" a woman's concerned voice rang out as she came into view. Her eyes grew wide in fear as she rushed to the child's side and snatched the pitchfork into her own petite hands. "Who are you?" she demanded while looking at Damian. She swung her weapon from side to side—from man to man.

Logan let out a low warning growl, but Damian held his left hand up in a gesture to quiet him. He didn't need his brother's temper hindering their quest for answers.

He looked steadily at the young woman and replied, "We are traveling through the area on our way into the Carpathian Mountains."

"Well then, I suggest you get going," she told him firmly.

He could hear her heart beating beneath her alabaster skin. It called to his appetite like a ringing dinner bell, and he imagined how pleasing she would be to his palate. He clenched his hands into balled up fists while he regained control of his senses.

"Or what?" Logan challenged the lass.

"I'll poke you full of holes, that's what," she spat, and he laughed heartily before his hand flew out and grabbed the pitchfork faster than the strike of a snake.

Damian flashed his brother a warning look. "Stop," he hissed while taking a protective step toward the woman and child, who was clinging to her dress. "We are not here to disrupt your lives. We merely seek answers that will help us find our father"—he breathed in slowly fighting every urge he felt to drink from her—"He has been missing since yesterday. Perhaps you've heard of him—he's King Lucian."

She had heard of him, he could tell, and she started to slowly back away. Still maintaining her poise, though, she said through gritted teeth, "He's not my king."

Logan growled again, but Damian just shrugged. "Well, that's not why we're here, so it's moot. We just want to know where he is."

"Would you know anything about that?" Logan interjected while surrendering the pitchfork back over to her.

"No, I surely would not," she answered haughtily while snatching back her weapon. She eyed them both suspiciously before finally laying it on the ground. "I'll ask you again to please leave."

Logan chuckled softly. "Tell us, wench, where is your husband? Perhaps he knows something."

"Humph, I doubt that. My husband is off to war, but don't think that there aren't men nearby who'll come to my rescue"—she watched them carefully—"All I have to do is scream."

Damian tilted his head at the brave woman, but Logan licked his jowls and sneered, "You do know who we are, don't you?"

She slanted her eyes at him. "Man or beast, I'll still put up a fight." She started to bend down for the pitchfork, but Damian held his hand up to stop her.

"We shall leave you be." He gave a meaningful look to Logan and nodded his head to the right. "We'll go this way."

THREE

The brothers walked around the quiet village until they saw smoke. The cook was an elderly woman, and she was basting a pig. Logan, like Damian, preferred his food to be alive when he dined, but Damian knew his brother was salivating from the smell of the roasting flesh.

Before Logan could pounce off and disrupt the woman's preparations, while destroying any chance they had of getting her to open up with any useful information, Damian put his hand on his twin's shoulder.

"Don't, Brother. Let her be," he said with authority. "We will catch more bees with honey."

Logan grunted in displeasure, but he acquiesced. The sound of the soft grass rustling beneath their heavy footsteps, along with the snapping of twigs, caught her attention, causing her to look up.

"Who are you?" she demanded while holding her hot poker up in self-defense.

Here we go again... "Madame, we come in peace from the kingdom of Drago. I am Damian Dragovich, son of King Lucian, and this is my brother, Logan."

Her narrowed black eyes shifted to Logan and back again. She held up a gnarled finger of her free hand and pointed at Damian.

"And what would the sons of a king be doing in our humble village? Are you here to plunder our meager homes too?"

Logan laughed at her absurdity, but Damian remained serious when he replied, "I assure you that the only thing we are seeking is answers. Our father has been taken, and we need to find him."

She searched their faces before finally lowering the hot poker and letting her guard down. "Well, if it is answers you seek from this village, then you stopped off at the wrong hut"—she held her finger up again, but she pointed west this time—"You need to find the old witch, Myna Magdelyn. She resides in the woods near the Carpathian Mountains."

"And she will help us?" Logan clenched his hands into balled up fists, which he often did when he was anxious.

The woman laughed and waved a hand at him. "Well, she can be of help to you, but that doesn't mean she will be. She's finicky that way."

"Explain," Damian demanded.

The woman wrung her knotted hands and took a deep breath. "Myna keeps to herself mostly. She rarely comes to the village, and she is peculiar in nature."

Logan was the one who laughed this time. "So is Damian."

She flashed a half-smile at the young werewolf and retorted, "Ah, but I expect he doesn't possess the gift of foresight or else he wouldn't be here. Am I correct in my guess?"

Her brief pause forced Logan to answer her. With a roll of his eyes and a gentle shrug, he quietly stated, "Aye."

Damian, getting more anxious with the passing of each minute, shifted his weight to his other foot causing some leaves to stir. "Enough. Is that true? Can she foretell the future?"

The woman's mouth pulled down, and she shrugged with both palms upward. "It is what I hear. But what do I know? I'm just an old woman." She cackled loudly and went back to her pig.

"Now what?" Logan inquired with a scowl. "Do we believe her story?"

Damian studied the woman for a minute longer before answering his brother. "Aye. We've nothing to lose but time, so let's get on with it. Head toward the mountains."

They began their walk in silence, but then Logan broke it when he asked, "Damian? Are you afraid of witches?"

Damian shot his twin a sideways glance and smiled broadly. "Are you serious? I'm a vampire, and you're a werewolf, so what do we need to be afraid of?"

Logan's face turned red before he spouted, "Well, yeah, but they know spells and shit."

Damian's belly rolled with laughter. "Are you afraid of being turned into a frog, Brother?"

Logan felt foolish for bringing the topic up, and he swiped his hand across his handsome face to hide his shame. Sheepishly, he mumbled, "I don't know, but we've never dealt with one before. Do you think she'll be able to help us?"

Damian pointed to a break in the trees. "I'm not sure, but we'll know soon enough—I can see her cottage about one hundred yards ahead."

FOUR

As the men approached the cottage door, it slowly creaked open to reveal a stunning woman, who looked nothing like the old crone they'd imagined. Before either brother could get a word out, she motioned for them to enter her abode.

"Come inside. I've been expecting you," she said in a less than enthused tone.

When she turned her back to them, Logan mouthed, "See?" to Damian, who was scratching his head in confusion.

"You were expecting us? Are you certain of that?" Damian asked the beautiful witch. "Are you Myna Magdelyn?"

She looked studiously at him and replied, "Yes, and I'm quite certain. You are brothers, are you not?" Damian nodded, and she continued, "And you are seeking something?"

This time he replied aloud, "Aye, we are looking for our father, but how do you know that?"

She laughed in a high-pitched cackle. "If you didn't know who I am, I expect you wouldn't be here, now would you?"

Logan stepped closer to her. "So, you have answers on our father's whereabouts then?"

She studied him carefully before sauntering over to a crude wooden table containing a skull, some bowls, candles, and a crystal ball. She took a pinch of leaves from one bowl and put them into another.

Impatient with her slowness and failure to reply, he pressed, "Well, do you?"

The witch looked up from her project with hooded eyes. "No, I don't know anything about your father. I knew you were coming, but I didn't know the exact reason why."

"But you said you knew we were seeking answers," Damian reminded her.

"Everyone who comes to see me is seeking answers. It's the only reason I get visitors."

"Well, can you provide them?" he inquired.

"Of course I can, but the question is do I want to? I mean what do I get out of it?"

Logan jingled his buckskin coin pouch, which was attached to his waist with a leather strap, and smiled. "We have gold. It's yours if you'll help us."

She cackled again. "Take a good look around boys. Does it look like that would do me any good out here?"

Logan started to advance toward her, but Damian grabbed his arm and stopped him. He didn't think going into battle with her was a good idea—there was an aura of pure evil surrounding the woman.

"Well, what will it take then?" Damian asked. "What will you accept as payment for your services?"

She sighed and sucked in her lower lip, which was full and ruby red, while pacing slowly around the small cottage. She eyed both brothers up and down but settled her hooded gaze upon Damian. "I'll let you know, but first things first."

Damian's brow furrowed. He knew that look—she was staring at him with lust blazing in her sultry eyes.

She slowly swayed her hips and strolled up to him, reaching out to trace a fingernail along his jawline. "Mmm," she purred sensuously.

Logan cleared his throat. "What are you going to do, witch? How can you help us find our father?"

Myna's eyes threw daggers at him for interrupting. In an irritated tone, she told him, "I have my ways. First, I'll consult the tea leaves."

She went to her table full of paraphernalia and dropped some leaves from one dish into another. She grabbed a kettle from the burning fireplace and poured hot water into the bowl, which she then swirled around before pouring the water out into a bucket on the floor. Her face contorted as she turned the bowl around several times, looking at it from different angles.

"What do you see?" Damian asked on a restless note.

"You are in for a long journey. It's one that will take several days."

"To where?" Logan demanded while moving closer to the table, so he could see what she was looking at.

"Your journey will lead you northwest of here to the other side of the mountains, and I don't expect it will be an easy one."

"That's all you have to say? Who took him? Who killed our mother?" Damian's questions came in rapid fire while he nervously paced the small quarters. He had counted on her being helpful, and now he wasn't feeling too confident that she would be. Furthermore, if there was a long journey ahead, they needed to get started on it as soon as possible. The more time spent at her cottage was more time their father would spend suffering—if he was still alive.

"Can you tell us more?" Logan asked impatiently with a huff. "Surely you have more answers for us than that."

"Calm down, boys. I didn't say I was done. There's more than one way to pluck a rooster." She put the bowl of leaves back on the table and sat down in front of her crystal ball. She waved one hand slowly over the ball, while the other clutched the necklace she wore, and began to chant in a foreign tongue.

Damian answered Logan's questioning stare with a shrug. He had no idea what she was saying either. He resumed pacing the small cottage, growing more agitated with each passing second. It was all he could do to keep from unleashing his temper on the witch. Then her voice stopped him in his tracks.

"I see a ring of fire and the spirit of a woman. She has silver-streaked blonde hair and emerald-green eyes," she said in a voice filled with mystery.

"That's our mother," Logan growled. "She was killed when our father was taken."

"She has a message for you," Myna continued.

"What is it?" Damian's brows shot up, and he quickly stepped closer to her with his hands clenching in fists.

The witch came out of her trance and leveled her gaze on him. "I'm going to let her tell you herself," she said.

"What are you talking about? You heard my brother, right?" Damian cocked his head in confusion.

She shrugged her small shoulders. "What? You've never heard of summoning the dead?"

"No, I haven't," he answered honestly.

She smiled while she lit three red candles sitting on her table. She put them in a triangular shape and then placed a lit white candle in the center. Next, she put a spotted feather into the flame of the white candle, and after it began to smoke, she dropped it into the bucket of water on the floor. Both men gaped at what they saw in the smoke—it was the transparent image of their mother.

"My sons," she greeted them, and her voice was just as clear as if she'd been standing in front of them. "It's good to see you and be seen by you."

A tear ran down Damian's sculptured cheek, and he murmured, "Mother, I'm so sorry we weren't there to protect you. I'm so sorry that we failed you."

"Aye," Logan added, "but we'll get our revenge."

Marisol Dragovich held her hand up to stop his rant. "You've not failed me. This isn't your fault, but you must find your father before he shares my fate."

"So, it's not too late then? He's still alive?" Damian asked with hope lining his voice.

"Yes, he's still alive," she answered calmly. "They knew that they would need him for leverage."

"Who? Who are you talking about? Who killed you and took Father?" Logan demanded.

"The Jackal clan did this," she said and held her arms out.

The men knew that the Jackals had been ostracized and banned from the kingdom of

Drago years before when their grandfather, King Titus, ruled because they couldn't be trusted.

Damian and Logan both spat multiple curses and growled. "We'll make sure that they pay!" Damian spat.

"Why? What do they want?" Logan interjected.

Their mother shrugged and shook her head. "I don't know what it is they are after, but I heard them say something to Lucian about the Hoia-Baciu Forest as I lay dying."

"The Haunted Forest?" Logan yelped and looked at his brother, who looked just as confused.

"Yes, and now I must go. Before I leave you, though, let me remind you that this was not your fault. Also"—she looked at her oldest son—"Damian, you need to let Logan lead once in a while and bear some of the burden."

"Aye," Logan sneered, causing his twin to scowl.

"Logan, you need to trust your brother's instincts," she chided him. "Separately, you both are very strong, but together, I'm sure you'll be unstoppable. Be good to each other and remember I love you." She blew them both a kiss and vanished.

Damian looked at Myna with deep gratitude. "Thank you for that, witch."

Myna waved one hand in the air. "It was nothing. It's just a trick a sorcerer taught me once."

"Well, we thank you nonetheless. Now, can you tell us about the forest?"

She pursed her lips and sighed while she carefully chose her words. "The Haunted Forest contains many secrets. I don't even know all of them. It is a sinister place if your intentions are wrong."

"You're being cryptic. What does that mean?" Damian questioned while walking around the room. His patience was too thin for riddles.

"Those who seek to take from the forest won't survive the shadows," she answered while fetching a book from a dusty shelf.

"You're still talking in circles, witch," Logan accused with anger etched on his face and in his voice. His patience always ran out before his brother's.

"There is magic hidden in the forest that even I can't comprehend. I don't know all that lies there because I can't get close enough to it—it's highly protected," she explained while flipping through the dusty book.

"What are you looking for?" Logan demanded.

She glanced up at him with a sparkle in her eyes. "I think there might be something in here about the forest, so try to show some patience." Her face grew serious, and her mouth turned into a pout while she searched through the book.

Logan looked to his brother for his reaction, and Damian just responded with one nod. It was his way of telling Logan to be patient and control his temper.

Myna suddenly broke the silence when she exclaimed, "Here it is. It says that, 'Only the man with the purest of heart and thoughts can seek the key hidden inside the forest. Only he can survive the tests to unlock the magic buried there. The guardians will destroy everyone else.' " She closed the book and looked up at the men. "That's it. That's all it says."

Logan stepped closer to her and asked on a growl, "What key? What are the tests?"

She only shrugged in response, but her smile was too mischievous to ignore.

Damian swiped his hand across his clenched jaw. "You mentioned a sorcerer earlier. Would he know more about the forest and what that riddle means?"

She cocked her head and scrunched her face in thought. "I suppose he might. You are free to seek his guidance, but I must warn you that he's not easy to get to. He's well protected inside a cavern that's hidden within the mountains, and it's a treacherous journey to get to it."

"I'm sure we can handle it," Damian calmly informed her.

She put her hands palm-up in front her and shrugged. "Suit yourselves. Go toward the highest peak of the mountains, where the winds gust the most, to find the cavern."

Logan dug into his leather pouch and pulled out several gold coins, which he offered to Myna. She held a hand up in protest, though.

"I told you that's not what I seek," she purred while she feasted her gaze on Damian once more.

Damian furrowed his brows under her scrutiny and asked, "What do you want then?" He had a feeling that he already knew the answer.

She slowly stepped toward him, swaying her hips in a seductive manner. "I want a taste at human life again. I want to feel the physical pleasures that I've been denied for too long out here in my solitude."

Damian unfolded his arms and took her by the shoulders to pull her closer to him in a rough manner. Then he ripped the top of her dress open to reveal her full bosom. He grabbed her left breast and squeezed while his mouth came down on hers hard.

In between rough kisses, he managed to growl, "This? This is what you desire?"

"Mmm, aye. This is what I want," she answered in a pant. Neither looked up when the door to the cottage slammed shut behind Logan.

Even though she was attractive, and he was aroused by her seduction, Damian didn't waste time with foreplay. Instead, he spun her around and drove himself into her dry heat. After he prodded her a few times, her passage became lubricated, allowing him deeper entry, and he brought her to pleasure twice before taking his own.

Afterward, he thanked her again and stepped outside to find Logan and start the next part of their journey.

Five

"Are you satiated now?" Logan grumbled while they headed toward the Carpathian Mountains.

"She wanted payment, so I didn't have much choice," Damian defended himself. "Who knows what kind of hocus-pocus she would've performed if I hadn't complied."

"Pfft," Logan scoffed, "you just couldn't pass up the chance to get pleasured."

"Whatever. Let's discuss what's important here—like what we can expect in the mountains."

Logan grinned, showing off his razor-sharp canines. "Mountain lions for dinner," he said salivating. He loved the physical challenge of taking down a strong predator.

Damian looked at him out of the corner of his eye and smiled too. "Okay, so the wildlife won't be a problem for us, but what about the weather?"

Logan mulled that over and responded, "We'll just have to try to keep moving or find a cavern to hole up in."

"Aye. What do you think he'll say about the Haunted Forest?"

Logan shook his head, and his smile turned down. "I don't know. I just hope he has something more useful to say than what the witch did, and I hope that he doesn't throw himself at you too." His grin returned with the last part.

Damian shot him a look of disapproval. "I found her to be quite helpful. She let us talk to Mother after all, and she told us about the Haunted Forest."

Logan scoffed, "You forgot to mention getting fucked."

Damian sighed but didn't bother to respond. He had the feeling that he wasn't going to live that down any time soon. A chill went down his spine when he recalled Myna's expression while she talked about the forest. He'd heard some stories about the legendary Haunted Forest, as it was nicknamed, and they weren't good. Even the witch admitted to not being able to explore the protected lands, and she had magic on her side. So, he wondered, what would that mean for the two of them?

They walked in silence, each lost in his thoughts, for over an hour. Then Logan announced, "I'm hungry. Let's stop and eat."

Damian felt pangs himself, so he agreed, "Aye, we can stop. Are you going to eat the pork or go hunting?"

Logan cocked a brow at his twin. Surely, he knew the answer to the question—naturally, he would hunt fresh prey. "I'll leave the pork for you. I prefer something a little more gamey," he said with a toothy grin. "If I cross paths with any nomads, I'll bring one back for you."

"I doubt you will, but okay. Try to make it a quick meal, so we can continue before dark."

Logan bobbed his head, undressed, and shifted into a werewolf. Damian watched as his brother pounced into the cover of the trees. Sometimes, he felt jealous that he'd been robbed of his true genetics by the vampires. He couldn't remember what it had felt like to embrace the wolf—wild and free—and it made him sad. He sat down and took the salt pork out of his knapsack. With a grimace, he bit off a large hunk and slowly chewed. He jumped when the stillness was pierced with a loud howl. It wasn't Logan's howl—it was the last fretful cry of the animal captured in his brother's steel-trap jaws.

The werewolf returned to the make-shift camp with a partially eaten mountain lion in its clutches. It sat on its haunches and consumed the rest of the large cat right down to the bone in just a matter of minutes, tearing the flesh with fangs and claws. He looked at Damian while licking the last bits of meat from his jowls and gave him a satisfied grin.

Damian wiped a hand across his face. He didn't particularly care to watch the beast eat. His method of dining was much more refined.

"Are you finished? Change and let's get going," he ordered. "Sundown is coming fast."

The werewolf looked up at the shadowy sky and shifted back into Logan's human form. He quickly redressed, and they packed everything up. They both looked at the steep and rocky hill they had to climb and frowned. It was going to be a long evening.

SIX

The twins made the treacherous climb, stumbling on occasion, well into the midnight hour when they finally found a cave to make camp in. The air had turned bitterly cold, and they only had small animal pelts to protect themselves from it.

"I think I'd be warmer if I changed," Logan suggested gruffly.

"Aye, you might be."

"Fuck it then; I will." Logan quickly undressed and turned himself back into the werewolf.

He rose on his back paws to his full height and shook his fur out. Logan never needed a full moon to change—he had the ability to transform on command whenever he desired to, just like his father. He hunkered down against the cavern wall and shot a meaningful look to Damian, who crossed the short distance between them and sat down on the other side of the beast to be blocked by the wind and enjoy the warmth of his thick fur. The werewolf closed its eyes, and soon its snores were echoing off the walls. Damian rested his head against the large beast and closed his eyes too, but it was difficult to fall asleep with the loud snoring.

They rested side by side for several hours until just before dawn. Damian was the first to wake up, so he nudged his brother. The wolf opened its eyes and lapped up the drool that was dripping from its fangs before looking at Damian.

"I'm hungry too," Damian said, reading his brother's expression. He took a hunk of stale bread out of his knapsack and began dining while Logan bounded off. *A vampire can't live like this. I need proper sustenance.*

After eating the bread and what was left of the salt pork, Damian paced the cave, waiting on Logan to return. It was almost twenty minutes before that happened, which only added to his already grouchy mood.

The werewolf entered the cavern, licking its chops, and caught the look of frustration on Damian's face. It quickly shifted back to human form before the vampire unleashed his wrath.

"I hurried up as fast as I could," Logan explained while dressing before Damian snapped at him.

"Did you catch another mountain lion, or was it a bear this time?" Damian asked trying to lighten his mood.

Logan scowled. "No, just a couple rabbits."

"Well, we might cross an eagle's nest on the way up."

"Pfftt, they aren't big enough to fill me."

Damian shook his head at his brother's ungratefulness. "Okay, how about a buzzard's nest then?"

Logan grinned. "That's better, but I'm hoping for a bear."

They grabbed their belongings and stepped out into the frigid air. Snow started to fall lightly at first as they made the trek, but then it got heavier and deeper and created an unpleasant suction around their buckskin boots as they weaved through the pine trees, getting closer to the top. It was good luck when they came across a cabin, and the mountain dweller was home. Damian feasted without hesitation, even though he preferred female blood, while Logan warmed in front of the fireplace and finished off the rabbit stew the man had been cooking. With their bellies full and warmed, they stepped out into the beginnings of a blizzard.

The heavy snow made their limbs numb and stung their eyes. Fortunately, they had found some warmer pelts and boots that fit in the nomad's cabin. Still, Mother Nature was winning the battle, and desperation began to settle in.

"Look!" Damian shouted over the gusty winds while pointing up the mountain. "I think that's it."

Logan squinted through the snowfall and saw a light that became a beacon of hope for both men. "I think you're right," he shouted back. "Let's go before I freeze my dick off!"

They stomped through the snow, which was holding on to their boots like glue, and thirty-five minutes that felt like days later, they were only twenty yards away from the cavern opening.

"What if he doesn't want to help us?" Logan pondered aloud.

"He has to or else we'll kill him," Damian replied with a scowl.

"But he has magical gifts."

Damian peered into his brother's concerned face. "First and foremost, he's a man, and all men have weaknesses."

Logan scowled at him. "Since when did you get all the answers?"

Damian couldn't help but laugh. "I just pay attention, whereas you're always out chasing butterflies," he jeered.

Logan shoved his shoulder, but he chuckled too if for no other reason than to help warm his blood.

With some hesitation, they approached the glowing cave entrance. It had an eerie blue light emanating from it, and the closer they got to it, the warmer they felt.

"What do you think that is?" Logan whispered.

Damian slowly shook his head. "I've no idea. Be alert though."

Logan rested his hand on the hilt of his dagger. "Oh, I am. Trust me, I am." He felt ready for anything. He'd never been a coward before, and he didn't want to be one now. Of course, magic was involved, and that worried him.

Damian stopped at the entrance, and his twin bumped into him. He shot the man a seething look over his shoulder.

"Be careful," he scolded, and Logan answered with a shrug.

Damian let the light splay on his face, basking in its warmth. He finally could feel his nose and lips again as they defrosted. Logan stepped forth so he, too, could warm up.

"Should we just go inside or knock?" Logan asked in a hushed voice.

Damian's brows shot up, and it was his turn to shrug.

Logan remembered what his mother had said—for Damian to let him lead occasionally, so he drew upon the strength of the werewolf and stepped forth into the glow.

"Hello?" His voice boomed and vibrated off the cavern walls. "Sorcerer?"

An even louder voice echoed back to them. "Who dares come here?"

Damian was the one who answered him. "We were sent by the witch, Myna Magdelyn. We've come from the kingdom of Drago to seek your help and guidance."

Silence followed for several seconds before the voice gruffly replied, "That kingdom no longer exists."

Damian felt the hairs on his neck stand on end—he was tired of people thinking that his father's legacy, his legacy, didn't exist anymore.

"We are the sons of Lucian Dragovich," he said with as much authority as he could muster.

Laughter rolled forth to them. "Well, why didn't you say so? Come on in."

SEVEN

The twins gave each other a quick glance and then stepped forth toward the source of the voice. The feeling of warmth grew as they entered the cavern, and their skin tingled as it defrosted. Oddly, though, the glow faded as they walked farther in, until it was replaced by the flicker of light coming from a fire.

An elderly man with a bald head and a long white beard sat before the blaze. He quickly looked up at the brothers and motioned for them to sit down.

"Welcome to my home, sons of Lucian," he greeted them with a smile. "I don't get much company here, so I'm glad you could visit."

Damian's brows knitted together while he studied the sorcerer. It was the oddest greeting he'd ever received.

"Thank you," he said, but it came out more as a question.

"Where did the blue glow disappear to?" Logan asked.

The sorcerer looked confused by the question. "What are you talking about, son?"

"The glow at the cave entrance. Where did it go?"

The wizard startled both men when he burst into raucous laughter. "I knew what you meant. I just wanted to see that look on your faces." He laughed some more and slapped his knee while the twins exchanged curious glances with one another. The sorcerer's eyes looked off into the distance, and he stroked his beard. "That light is a mystery to all, including me, much like the Aurora Borealis. It's actually how I found this cavern, and in all these years, I haven't figured out the source of its magic."

Damian studied the man, wondering if he was joking with them again. The wizard caught him staring, though, and raised a brow at him.

"You're the oldest, aren't you?"

Damian nodded. "Aye, I am."

The sorcerer eyed Logan carefully. "And you're the wild one between the two of you. You have a short temper and are more connected to the wolf than most in your bloodline."

Logan's face scrunched up. "Am I? I didn't know that."

The wizard nodded. "You are indeed. Now, what brings you to the mountain?"

Damian cleared his throat and answered for them, "As I said before, the witch sent us. She said if anyone could help us, it would be you. We are looking for our father, who was taken by the Jackal clan. Our mother's spirit told us that she heard mention of the Haunted Forest while she was dying."

The sorcerer nodded in understanding. "So, you want to know about the Cursed Forest. You are curious about the magic within, am I right?"

Both men nodded and noticed that the man's hands were trembling as he stoked the fire.

"The secret mysteries of the Hoia-Baciu Forest are not to be taken lightly. I first learned of the Cursed Forest from my mentor before he

passed"—he threw another log onto the fire—
"and he told me about the sacred treasure allegedly
hidden within its folds." He looked at the twins to
make sure they were paying close attention before
he continued. "You're no doubt wondering about
this treasure too. In fact, I'm sure that's what the
Jackals seek."

"Well, what is it?" Logan pressed.

The wizard put his finger to his lips to hush
the young werewolf. "It's the most unbelievable
and coveted thing in the world, if it in fact exists.
No one has been able to prove it and lived to tell
about it."

The wizard's story completely engrossed
the brothers. While he paused his story to take a
drink, Logan threw another log onto the fire for
him.

"Go on. What is supposedly there?" he
encouraged the sorcerer.

The wizard met their gazes, swallowed
another sip, and held his crude cup in the air.
"Would you like some ale? I have plenty," he
offered.

Both brothers were parched, so they
eagerly accepted the cups offered to them. The
brew had a strange sweet smell, but it was delicious
nonetheless.

"Now, where was I? Oh, yes. The treasure
of the woods"—he stared deeply into the dancing
flames of the fire, watching the flickers of light
performing before their eyes—"Allegedly, mind
you, the forest hides and protects a forbidden
spring."

"What's so special about a spring?"
Damian scoffed, and the sorcerer scowled at him.

"It grants eternal life—that's what's so special," he stated firmly.

The twins quickly looked at each other with raised brows. "The Jackals," they said in unison.

"They want the spring," Damian finished the shared thought. "They want immortality too." The Jackals, they knew, aged at a normal rate and, thus, didn't survive as long as werewolves or vampires. It's one reason the tribes didn't get along. Territory rights was another.

The wizard slowly nodded. "Many have wanted the spring, and many have disappeared while trying to find it."

Logan stood up and paced the circle they were sitting in. "Isn't it just a matter of making it through the forest to find it? The witch said it was dangerous, but we're no strangers to peril."

Damian shot his brother a look to make him stop talking. "Go on. Please tell us why people disappear, and have you ever been inside it? The witch said she didn't get very far, but she obviously survived."

The sorcerer nodded again. "Yes, I've been inside the forest."

"And you're okay," Logan interrupted.

"Am I? I'm not so sure about that. You see, when I entered the forest, I was a young apprentice, but when I emerged from the woodland"—he looked down while gesturing to his body—"I was this." His right hand coiled his beard around it while he gazed from vampire to werewolf. "Time had passed for me, yet for the world, it hadn't."

"What happened to you in there?" Damian asked on a shaky voice.

The wizard shrugged, though. "That's one of my troubles. I simply don't know." He saw their confusion, so he elaborated. "There are things about the forest I can recall, but then there is a huge chunk that I cannot. I woke up on the forest floor, having no idea why I'd passed out, or why I looked like this."

Logan sighed heavily, and Damian whispered, "Interesting. The forest aged you somehow."

The sorcerer nodded and refilled their cups with more of the sweet ale.

"So, what can you remember about the place? What are we up against?" Damian continued.

"Why didn't the witch age?" Logan added to his brother's questions.

The wizard cocked his head slightly and once again stared into the fire as if it was whispering the answers to him. Then, with a wave of his hand, the flames grew even though there wasn't much wood left for it to burn.

"Here's what I recall," he started to explain. "The air hangs like a grim evil and almost cuts off your breath while it whispers secret terrors to you. It was almost like I could hear a woman's voice telling me to beware and telling me to leave at once. Then there are the trees, which are like nothing you've ever seen before. Terrified faces are screaming at you from the bark of the trees. It's as if wanderers had been absorbed into the wood and are trying to warn you. I can remember always feeling like someone or something was watching my every move, but I didn't see the source—not even one squirrel or other forest dweller. Sometimes, out of nowhere, I'd see a light, but I could never locate the source." He took a deep breath and a sip of his drink. "That's it. I blacked out, and when I woke up, I was at the edge of the woods, looking as I do now."

"The Jackals won't be able to go in if it ages you," Logan suddenly said, piercing the silence. "But it shouldn't affect us much."

The wizard shook his head and lowered his eyes. "Don't you understand that your lives are at risk if you go into the forest? Don't you know people completely disappear inside the woods as if they were swallowed whole by the evil lurking there?"

Logan blurted out, "But our father's life is at risk, and if we drink from the spring, then we'll truly be immortal, and the Jackals won't be able to defeat us."

The wizard held a hand up to give the young wolf pause. "There's one more thing about the rumored spring. It's not just a matter of finding it. There is only one thing that opens it, and that is the legendary Fire Opal."

"Where do we find it?" Damian inquired.

The wizard laughed softly. "If it exists, then it will only be found in the Cursed Forest, and I can assure that it will be well-protected by something."

"We've been warned," Logan grumbled. "We'll leave in the morning."

Damian nodded once. "Aye, in the morning."

The wizard wiped his hand over his long beard again while shaking his head vigorously. "May the gods be with you then."

EIGHT

Damian and Logan slept for a few hours and were up as soon as the sun rose. The wizard had fixed a light repast for them, and even Logan ate some of it because there weren't decent hunting grounds in the area, which made him question the wizard.

"How do you survive here? Even I don't have a decent place to hunt."

The sorcerer laughed. "Magic, young wolf, it's all about magic. I can conjure what I need to survive in my humble home"—he gestured to the expanse of the cavern—"In fact, I fabricated some bread and sweet meats for you to take on your journey, and here's a flask of water too." He put his finger to his chin and glanced in the direction of the cavern entrance. "The pelts you brought aren't nearly enough to protect you from the bitter elements—I'll remedy that for you." He closed his eyes and chanted in another language. Suddenly, pelts and boots made from thick rabbit fur appeared before the brothers. "These will keep you warm."

Damian, who was already packing the food and water, smiled at the wizard with appreciation. "I offer you our sincere thanks, but I feel you deserve more, so here is some gold too." He reached out with a fistful of gold pieces, but the sorcerer waved it off.

"I've no need for it," he said.

"Well, how can we repay you for your kindness and for the information you gave us? I feel like we need to do something for you, starting with learning your name," Damian pressed.

The wizard laughed. "I guess we never did get that far, did we? My name is Garron."

Damian smiled at the man. "That's Gaelic, isn't it?"

"You are correct," Garron answered with a twinkle in his mysterious eyes. He looked at Logan, who was dressing in the pelt and boots. "I wish you'd reconsider going into that dreadful forest."

Damian drew a deep breath. "I understand your concern, and I appreciate it, but if Logan and I are to succeed at rescuing our father, we'll need to find the Fire Opal and the spring. Otherwise, the two of us won't be able to defeat the Jackal clan."

Garron stared into the fire. "Build an army—the Jackals must have other enemies you can reach out to. We can use magic as well. I'll find a spell that will help. I'm sure there's something useful for us"—he looked up at Damian with sadness in his eyes—"You two are the first people to visit me in at least twelve years, and I'd hate to lose my new friends."

Even Logan smiled at the kind wizard. "We would hate that also, but we'd hate to lose our father even more. We have to move quickly to save him," he replied.

Damian, who'd been staring into the fire himself, added, "I agree, and there isn't time to spare. We have to try to find the spring."

"Let's get going now, Brother," Logan announced. "We have a long journey."

"Aye, that we do. Thank you again, Garron, for your assistance. It means more to us than you'll ever know."

"Just save King Lucian and help him rebuild your kingdom. That will be repayment enough for me—I might even come down off my mountain," he said with a grin.

"Will do," Damian promised and waved good-bye as he followed Logan in the direction of the cavern entrance.

The freezing wind didn't bite as much through the new pelts, so the trip down the northeast side of the mountain didn't seem like it would be as bad. When they entered the forest, they crossed paths with a large black bear, and it attacked before Logan had the chance to shift. It managed to swipe Damian's arm, leaving a shallow gash, before the vampire wrapped his strong arms around it and tackled it to the ground.

Talk about a bear hug...

The werewolf was rushing up behind Damian and the thrashing creature, so Damian rolled out of the way, giving the fierce beast room to pounce on the bear. It sank its teeth into the black bear's throat while its claws did the rest of the work. The bear shrieked the awful sound of a surprising death into the still air, and it made Damian cringe. He was a killer, but it was normally in a silent manner. It was never this vicious.

After Logan had his lunch, they followed the sun west until they were standing on the edge of the Hoia-Baciu Forest. They tried to peer inside, but dense bushes and trees made it difficult to see much.

"Do you hear that?" Damian asked.

"I don't hear anything," Logan responded, straining to listen.

"Exactly. There aren't any bird noises or anything."

"Garron told us that he never saw any creatures," Logan reminded him while stepping closer to the forest.

"I know, and that just worries me that his entire story was true."

Logan looked at his brother over his shoulder. "Did you really think he was lying to us?"

Damian's mouth turned down, and his eyes looked down at his boots. "No, and that's why I'm worried. What if we can't get to the spring?"

Logan shrugged and kept inching closer to the tree line. "We have to try. Father would risk his life for us."

Damian's scowl and frown lines deepened. "I know he would, and of course we will for him. I just have to pause and wonder if there is another way."

Logan shook his head and popped his knuckles. "If you thought there was another way, you should've said so when we were with Garron. He offered to help us. Now isn't the time for self-doubt, Brother."

Damian sighed and bobbed his head while staring at the mysterious forest. "You're right. There isn't any other way, so let's proceed."

Mustering all their courage, they entered the Haunted Forest to face the unknown sinister forces waiting for them.

nine

King Lucian slowly lifted his feeble head when he heard the rattle of keys followed by the creaking and moaning of the door on its rusty hinges. The jackal guard entered with a bowl of food and some water, which he tossed down on the dirt floor in front of the king before leaving without a word.

Lucian looked at the fish and burnt bread and wrinkled his nose. If he hadn't been denied the last two meals, he would've pushed it away. Instead, he used both dirty hands to feed himself and then drank all the water. He closed his eyes and prayed to be rescued soon. He knew his sons were looking for him, but he didn't know if they were aware of where to look. He also didn't know how long it would be before Gortock, ruler of the Jackal clan, ordered his death. He heard the rattle of keys again, and this time, two guards entered with Gortock behind them.

"Well, well," Gortock began with a menacing sneer, "how are we enjoying our stay?"

Lucian looked away from the ruler and didn't respond. That earned him a kick from one of the guards, who growled, "You look at Gortock and answer when spoken to."

"Very well," Lucian hissed. "To what do I owe this immense displeasure?" That earned him another kick, which was harder than the one before, and when he moaned in pain, all three jackals laughed.

"Are you ready to make this easier on yourself? You know, I can make your stay here more comfortable. I will even let you go, but you know what I need," Gortock hissed. "Just tell me the location of the Fire Opal and how to get it."

Lucian shook his head. "I'll never tell you."

The guard was about to strike him again, but Gortock held up a hand to stop him.

"I think another punishment is more befitting a king. Bring in the thumbscrew."

ten

The brothers entered the creepy forest with their hands on the hilts of their swords and their eyes looking all around. It was deathly quiet, and the air hung heavy.

"We need to move quickly before it gets dark. Well, darker," Damian said. It was already difficult to see because of the thick vegetation—the treetops were almost blocking out the sun altogether.

Logan stumbled on a tree root. "I'm not going to argue with you"—he pointed ahead of them—"The wizard was right about the trees."

Damian looked at the trees, which were bent in a bizarre fashion, and a coldness settled in the pit of his stomach. "Yes, he was. I've never seen anything like this."

"Look there," Logan exclaimed while pointing. "Do you see what I'm seeing?"

"If you mean the faces in the tree, then yes." Another chill ran down Damian's spine and made his body shake. "Keep moving."

Logan picked up the pace, but he was still on edge. "How's your arm?" he asked with concern.

Damian's concentration on the forest had made him forget all about the wound inflicted by the bear. "It stings when I pay attention to it, but at least it stopped bleeding."

"That's good. How far do you think we'll have to go to find the spring?"

Damian looked at him and shrugged. "I'm not sure, but if you recall, we have to find the Fire Opal first."

"Oh yeah," Logan replied while bobbing his head. "What do you think that is?"

"I don't know."

"Well, if we don't know what we're looking for, then how are we going to find it? Also, how big is this forest?"

Damian sighed with exasperation. "Logan, I don't know, okay? I don't have any answers. I just hope we'll stumble across it."

Logan faltered over vegetation again. "We really didn't think this through, did we?"

Damian answered only with a shake of his head. Then both jumped as a chilly wind blew past with a feminine voice demanding, "Get out!"

Logan stared into his twin's eyes. "You heard that too, didn't you?"

Damian nodded but found himself choked off from words. Cold terror, colder than the wind that had blown past them, gripped his heart in its icy embrace and squeezed. He wondered what in hell they were doing there.

Logan took slow, hesitant steps forward as a wave of apprehension washed over him. His heart was hammering inside his chest, and he found it difficult to breathe.

"Damian, I feel like we're being watched," he whispered.

Damian's eyes were shifting left to right. "Aye, I can feel it too." With slowly mounting dread, he continued to walk forward. They made it several feet before the voice returned.

"Get out now!" the female voice shouted louder this time.

Damian froze in his tracks and shouted back, "Who's there? We are not here to hurt you or the forest."

"What are you doing?" Logan scolded him on a loud whisper.

Damian scrunched his brows and called out, "We need help." He stopped walking and waited to see if the voice would respond. Logan slowly approached him, his feet snapping twigs on the forest floor.

"What are you doing?" he repeated.

Damian opened his mouth to reply, but he quickly snapped it shut when he heard rustling in the foliage. Something was coming. He exchanged a nervous glance with Logan and tightly gripped his dagger. Then something unexpected stepped through the trees—a small female dressed in a green gossamer shift.

"Why are you here?" she demanded in an exotic voice filled with authority.

Damian relaxed his grip on his weapon—he felt no need to be afraid of this petite female. "We are the sons of King Lucian, who has been abducted by the Jackal clan, and we need to find the Fire Opal to save him."

Her eyes grew wide but remained guarded. "The Fire Opal? Few know of its existence. How did you learn about it?"

"We were told about it by the wizard, Garron, who lives in the mountains," Damian replied. "We have reason to believe that the Jackal clan is after it, and that's why they took our father."

Logan added, before she could reply, "Do you know where it is?"

She eyed them one at a time before calmly answering, "I know everything about this forest, including its dangers. What do you know about the Fire Opal, though?"

Damian felt all his senses on edge. He had the feeling there was more to this mysterious woman than what they saw, and he didn't want to underestimate her. Logan, on the other hand, was just as impulsive as ever. He unsheathed his weapon and pointed it at her.

"What do you know about it, and where is it?" he demanded.

"Logan!" Damian eyed his brother and spoke sharply, "We are guests in this forest, so act like it."

Logan took the look from his brother seriously and sheathed his weapon. He remained on guard though. He didn't trust the wench.

Damian bowed his head toward the female. "My apologies for my brother's behavior. To answer your question, we know that the Fire Opal opens the Sacred Spring."

Her tone immediately turned aggressive. "Who are you? Why do you want to find the spring?"

Damian cocked his head, ignoring Logan's snort, and calmly replied, "We are Damian and Logan Dragovich, sons of King Lucian Dragovich. We've been told that the spring grants eternal life. We need to drink from it in order to defeat the Jackal clan's army."

She was about to say something but paused. "You are telling me the truth, and that is rare. I can tell you are noble at heart, and that is also rare when it comes to the people who enter these woods"—she squinted her eyes—"You aren't a mortal, though, are you?"

"No, I'm a werewolf-turned-vampire, and my brother is a werewolf. May I ask who and what you are?"

She relaxed her stance and replied, "I'm Valen, guardian of the woods, and I'm a wood nymph."

Damian smiled at her. "It's nice to meet you, Valen. Now that we've been introduced, can you help us? Will you help us find the Fire Opal?"

She studied him carefully and slowly approached. He froze in place when she reached out a delicate hand to touch his face. He even held his breath until his lungs screamed. Out of the corner of his eye, he saw Logan tense up and reach for his weapon, so he held a hand up to halt him. Even though she appeared feminine and frail, he had the feeling she was anything but, because how could something delicate survive in the Haunted Forest?

"Interesting," she whispered in soothing hushed tones.

"What is?" he dared to ask.

She stared into his dark eyes, and he noticed hers were a startling violet. "That you were turned. I've never heard of that happening"—she looked at his full lips and instinctively ran her tongue over hers—"And I've never met a vampire or werewolf before either." She dropped her hand and approached Logan, who was still tensed up. "Relax, werewolf, if I wanted to hurt you, I would've already done so."

Logan's belly rolled with laughter. "You hurt us? Do you really believe that's possible?"

Valen's mouth twitched and turned into a slight frown right before she grabbed his wrist, flung him over her shoulder to the ground, and put his dagger to his throat. He tried to grab her, but vines magically entwined around his wrists and ankles before he could.

Damian's raucous laughter made both of them glance his way. He was doubled over, clutching his stomach, and his face had turned just as red as his brother's. "I think she won that fight, dear Brother."

Logan growled in humiliation before tensing up under her fingertips—she ran her hand over his face too. "Do you mind?" he mumbled with shame.

She giggled softly. "Release," she ordered, and the vines retreated. "You're both magnificent," she said with admiration but took a few steps away from him. She looked at Damian, who was rubbing his injured arm, and told him, "I can help you with that wound."

He looked down at his arm and then back at her. "How?"

She opened her arms wide and gestured to the vegetation around them. "This is a magical forest. You already know that, or you wouldn't be here."

"Are there other magical elements besides the spring?" Logan asked.

She nodded vigorously, and her smile seemed to light up the darkness around them. "Yes, lots."

"Will you help us then? Will you take us to the Fire Opal?" Damian inquired while stepping closer to her. She was bent down, collecting leaves from the forest floor.

Valen stood, reached out with leaves covered with soil, and pressed it to his wound. "Apparently, you don't know the entire story."

"Excuse me?"

She glanced up from his arm. "There is more to the story about the Fire Opal than what you've heard. I can't just give it to you. It's well-protected—even I can't touch it."

"So then why is there a spring if no one can get to it? Why even bother protecting it?"

"Because there is one who can get to it. It lies in wait for the chosen one," she said cryptically.

"Well, who is this special one?" Logan asked with irritation punctuating his words.

"The only clue I have to his identity is that he's the first son of the first son," she answered softly. "Now, we need to go before it's completely dark, and the forest is hard to navigate."

"Do we have anything to worry about? Any unforeseen dangers?" Damian asked while following her into the brush.

She threw him a glance over her shoulder and gave him a secretive smile. "Not if you're with me."

eleven

The jackal guard returned with the torture device and a small table, which he placed in front of King Lucian.

Gortock stepped closer to him and sneered, "Are you sure you don't want to tell me where the Fire Opal is? You could make this so much easier for yourself."

Lucian threw daggers at the jackal with his eyes while digging deep inside himself once more, to find the strength to shift. If only he could become the wolf, he might stand a chance. He used his hatred as the fuel to make the change, but nothing happened—he was too weak, and he was out of practice. It was his fault for not regularly making the shift—it had been several months since he'd turned into the beast. He didn't think it was proper for a refined king to sprout fur and fangs. Now, though, he'd give his left nut if he could make the change.

"Suit yourself then," Gortock mumbled and motioned to the guards.

One jackal approached and straddled over him to pin him against the wall. Lucian struggled, but it did him no good—the creature was too strong. The second guard pushed the table toward Lucian, grabbed his right hand, and placed his forefinger into the device.

"This is called the thumbscrew. I'm sure you can imagine what it does," Gortock said in an amused tone. "Proceed," he ordered, and the guard cranked the device to make it crush down on Lucian's finger. Lucian screamed in agony as the bones in his finger were crumbled.

"Now, let's try this again," Gortock hissed. "Where is the Fire Opal, and how do I get it?"

Lucian's breaths were coming in ragged pants, but he managed to gasp, "I won't tell you." He couldn't—it would put Damian's life at risk, and also, if the Jackal clan got access to the mystical spring, they'd overtake all the lands after killing both of his sons. He'd rather endure the torture and accept his death than put his sons at risk. If the twins got access to the spring first, then they would be invincible and could rescue him. This is what he was holding out hope for.

"Break every finger on that hand," Gortock growled with frustration before storming out of the cell.

The guard stared into the feeble king's eyes as he put the rest of his fingers into the crushing device and turned the handle. Piercing cries rang out through the cell bars to the other prisoners, who sobbed in fear and sympathy for the king.

TWELVE

The twins followed Valen through the brush, and then found themselves in a meadow filled with an assortment of huge flowers.

"This is it," she announced and gestured to the open area. "This is where I live."

Logan stared at her like she had just grown a third arm. "How can you live here?" He, too, gestured to the meadow. "Where is your house?"

She smiled and pointed to a huge tree. "I live in that tree, but I usually sleep under the flowers."

Damian chuckled and chimed in at that point, "While the flowers are bigger than what I'm used to seeing, there's no way you fit under them."

Valen giggled. "Sure there is. It works like this." She reached out to touch one of the daisies, and the flower suddenly grew to enormous proportions. Then she snuggled underneath it. "See?"

The twins stared in amazement at her display of magic. "That's quite a gift you have," Damian commented.

She shrugged like it was no big deal. "It's one of them. I'm the keeper of the forest, so it treats me well."

Logan sat down with his legs crossed. "Are the stories true? Is the forest haunted?"

She tilted her head and sighed while clasping her hands in her lap. Damian took a seat next to his brother, so she was now facing both men. "If I tell you, that takes away from the mystery of the forest. I will tell you, though, that people have died here."

Damian scowled, but Logan pressed her, "Really? That's all you're going to say?"

Valen gave him a little nod but no verbal answer.

"Will you tell us why there are faces in the trees, or why they are bent that way?" Logan continued the inquisition.

She pretended to think about it but shook her head no. "I'll tell you this much—if you're hungry, you can eat the flowers."

Logan rolled his eyes and threw his hands up in the air. "Gee, that's helpful for a werewolf and a vampire. Any other bright ideas?"

She got up, approached them, and reached for two flowers, which she used her magic touch on. They, too, grew to tower over the men.

"I don't think we need those, but thanks," Damian said.

"You might think differently when the storm comes," she forewarned while sitting back down under the flower.

The brothers both looked up at the sky, which they could now see, and saw streaks of lightning making creases. The rumble of thunder followed each flash, and the trees began to sway in a heavy breeze. The first large, gray drops of rain began to slowly fall, but it wasn't long before the pace increased, and the ground grew drenched around them. Although they didn't understand how, the flowers were keeping them dry. With their knees pulled into their chest, they watched the sky in the distance, and as the storm raged, the lighting struck closer each time. The fury of the squall subsided after ten minutes of lashing out, though, and all was once again quiet.

"Why aren't there any animals in the forest?" Logan blurted out.

Valen looked around them and replied in a whisper, "It's because of the air. There's something in the air that keeps them away."

Damian nodded with understanding. "It's dismal and heavy," he acknowledged.

"Yes," she softly replied, still looking around like she expected something to jump out at them.

"How do you survive it then?" Logan pondered.

Valen shrugged her small shoulders. "I just do. The forest needs someone to protect it, so I'm safe."

He accepted her answer but wondered, "What about us? Are we going to be okay?"

Her nose wrinkled up. "You're okay now, aren't you?"

"Aye."

"Get your rest, and we'll talk more about things at sunup," she advised.

The twins dug into their knapsacks for the food and water provided by Garron. It wasn't what they preferred, but they made do for the time being. They closed their eyes and followed Valen into the dream realm.

Damian was dreaming about his parents at first, but then he was whisked away to another lucid dream filled with sexual desire. He felt the gentle stroke of Valen's hand on his cheek, tingling beneath her fingertips, followed by her hot breath as she stood on her tiptoes to kiss him. He accepted her kiss, and their tongues silently danced in the warm cave of her mouth. Then he broke the kiss off and nuzzled his way across her cheek to gently bite her earlobe.

She took his fingers into her mouth and teased them with her tongue before sucking on them. Growing crazy with desire, Damian's teeth raked her neck while a lusty feeling of warmth stole over him, causing him to grow diamond-hard. Then, so he wouldn't bite her, he pulled back and stared into her hazy purple eyes.

"Are you sure about this?" he whispered with his voice dripping with lust. "Are you sure you want to bed a vampire?"

Valen's hand ran down the hardness of his chest and abdomen and then played over his groin. "I'm sure that I want you."

"That's all I need to hear."

His breath was once again hot on her neck, but then it trailed downward over her collar bone and just above her bosom. His hands went to work on her dress, pushing it downward to her waist, while his kisses landed hot and heavy over her flesh when it became exposed. She made a gasping noise as he took her pink peak into the inferno of his mouth and suckled. Her breasts were ripe, succulent mouthfuls for Damian, and he enjoyed each one fully while the heavy heat grew between his legs. The intensity of his erection became overwhelming, though, and he needed to find release within her walls, so he tugged on the dress until it was gone. While she stood nude before his greedy gaze, he worked his own clothing until he was fully exposed as well.

They knelt together before he gently laid her on her back. He parted her thighs and found her wet, ready, and silently begging for him. He briefly paused at her hot opening before pushing his heavy erection inside. She wrapped her legs tightly around his powerful frame and rested her hands on his forearms while he dove in and out of her molten center. Blinding pleasure was just a few strokes away for them, and they raced toward it together. Friction on friction, they pummeled each other to the edge and then toppled over into oblivion.

"Wake up, Damian," Logan's voice disturbed his afterglow. "It's morning, and we need to continue our journey."

Thirteen

Reluctantly, Damian left his wonderful dream and opened his eyes. Logan was studying his face. "What? Why are you staring at me?"

Logan shook his head, and his long hair moved around his handsome face. "Just wondering what you were dreaming about, but I bet I can guess based on the moaning and groaning sounds you were making"—he pointed to Damian's groin—"and of course there's that."

Damian quickly covered his erection with his knapsack since Valen was right there and pretended to look through it. *Valen. I can't face her.* When he looked up, he noticed the trees and flowers around them. After last night's storm, everything appeared more lush and vibrant. Even the air had changed—it was lighter and cleaner. The forest looked like a regular woodland instead of the grim place they had entered yesterday.

Valen must have read his mind because she broke the silence when she stated, "It looks different doesn't it?"

He shook his head vigorously. "It's like night and day."

Valen looked around, too, with a smile gracing her shimmery sun-kissed lips, and for the first time, he noticed the shiny highlights in her blonde hair. His eyes wandered down her frame, while she was still looking away, and settled on her delicate feminine curves. Tightness pulled at his groin again, so he had to look away from her. He couldn't let his waking mind go there.

"Are you ready?" she suddenly asked and startled him.

"Ready?" Damian repeated. "Oh, you mean to finish the journey? Yes, I'm ready." He looked around again at the opulent forest before meeting the watchful stare of his twin. "What?"

Logan looked at Valen and then back to Damian with a slight grin. "Nothing. Nothing at all. Let's just go."

Damian rolled his eyes. They were twins, but there were times when he wasn't sure that they came from the same womb. "Valen, are you going to take us to the Fire Opal?"

Her face twisted, and she bit her lower lip before responding, "It's like I told you yesterday, I can't touch it. I know where it is because I am to protect it along with the forest, but according to the legend, only the first son of the first son can touch it."

"I'm the first son of the first son, but surely there are others who fit that description as well," Damian said, frustrated.

Valen's perfect brows shot up, and she informed him, "Well, there is a second part to the prophecy. It is said that the chosen one also bears a unique birthmark."

Damian's heart raced with excitement. "Do you mean like this?" He pulled up his shirt and pulled his waistband down just enough to reveal a birthmark in the shape of a star on his hip.

Valen studied the unusual mark with wide eyes. "That might be it," she said, her voice filled with excitement.

"There's one way to find out," Logan interrupted their exchange, "so let's get on with it."

Valen pointed west. "We're going this way." She started off with the twins close behind. "Be careful where you step because the vines may try to grab you."

"There's a lovely thought," Logan grumbled.

Damian didn't say anything. He was too mesmerized by the sway of Valen's hips and the delicate curve of her buttocks.

Logan caught him staring and grumbled, "Just take her and get it over with."

"I will not," Damian hissed. He was hungry though. He needed blood, and he needed the company of a woman. Once he got out of the forest, he'd hunt for both.

When they stepped back into the woodland, it turned sinister again. The air was thicker, and the trees seemed to be reaching for them. "Do you see this?" Logan whispered.

"Do you mean the change in the ambiance? Yes, I noticed it." Damian, too, looked around half expecting something to jump out at them.

Valen had overheard them and turned around to tell them, "You can't turn your back on the forest. She is fickle like a Venus fly trap—pretty on the outside but dangerous if you get too close."

Damian narrowed his eyes on her. "What other dangers can we expect?"

"Yes, what aren't you telling us?" Logan pointed a finger at her to punctuate his words.

She brushed a stray lock of blonde hair away from her gossamer skin and looked away from their inquisitive stares. "Well, there are sink holes, so watch for those in addition to groping vines, and don't aggravate the spirits."

The twins quickly glanced at each other before Damian asked, "The spirits? What do you mean? You said there were no ghosts."

She gently shook her head. "No, if you recall I simply told you people have died here. Sometimes, the forest keeps them from moving on."

Damian held a finger up to interrupt her. "How and why? And what do you mean by aggravate them? How would we do that?"

Her shoulders lifted and fell in a deep sigh. "I don't know how because I don't know all of the mysteries of the forest either. I simply protect it from intruders, and I care for the vegetation. When I said don't aggravate them, I simply mean don't disrupt the plants or trees—they get angry. Now, to keep you safe, I think it's best we finish our journey and get you out of the forest."

They continued walking in silence for a few minutes when Logan suddenly cried out. A vine had grabbed him by the ankle, causing him to fall on his face, and it dragged him helplessly across the ground.

"Damian, do something!" He struggled with all his strength to get away, but the more he resisted, the more entangled he became. Damian ran to catch up with his dagger drawn, and Valen wasn't far behind him.

"Release him!" she commanded, but the vines were merciless, and suddenly, they were pulling him into a sink hole.

Damian hacked at the vine while Valen grabbed Logan's hand and pulled. Damian's dagger couldn't penetrate the skin despite his efforts, so he flung himself onto the vine to sink his fangs in and try to tear it. The skin was too tough for his incisors, though, too.

"Grab his hand," Valen shouted at him and gestured with her head. "Do it now!"

Damian lunged forth and grabbed Logan's free hand that was clawing at the ground. He pulled as hard as he could, knowing that he might dislocate his brother's arm, while Valen let go of the other hand and sprung toward Logan's restrained ankles. She pressed her hand to the vine and again ordered it to release the young werewolf. There was a loud snapping sound, and Logan's massive frame flew forward after he was released. The vine retreated into the thick underbrush.

Logan's panting was loud and raspy as he used his hands to pull himself farther away from the hole. Damian reached out and grabbed his arm to assist him while Valen crept softly to them.

"I'm sorry about that. I warned you, but still, I'm sorry. As I said, the forest is finicky."

"The forest is a bitch!" the werewolf growled harshly.

Valen tilted her head and gazed at the heavily wooded area. "Well, the good news is the resting place for the Fire Opal is just over the next hill."

FOURTEEN

The throbbing in Lucian's hand was finally giving way to a blissful numbness, so he lay down on the hard dirt floor, closed his eyes, and tried to rest. It took several minutes, but sleep finally took hold and pulled him into the kingdom of dreams. However, they were fitful imaginings. He pictured his sons fighting their way through the Haunted Forest to find the Fire Opal. The tormented spirits protecting the woodland challenged every move they made, though, and threw them off the right path, and soon, they became lost and disoriented.

"Wake up!" Gortock interrupted his dream by kicking his injured hand.

Lucian bellowed in excruciating pain, which caused an eruption of laughter from the merciless leader and his guards.

"Let me be," the weakened king pleaded.

Gortock smiled maliciously. "Now, you know I can't do that. I won't do that unless you tell me what I want to know. Give me the information, and I assure you that we'll leave you alone. You have my word."

Lucian sneered, "Your word means nothing to me. I would sooner trust the word of a snake."

Gortock put his clawed hand to his chin and rubbed. "You know, there are ways to loosen your tongue. Allow me to demonstrate." He motioned to one of the guards who then left the cell.

A few minutes later, the guard reappeared with a tongue clamp in his hand and another prisoner in tow.

"Show him," Gortock commanded.

The prisoner realized what was going to happen and struggled to bolt for it, but the second guard was quick—he struck the man down with a crushing blow to his shoulder. The condemned man writhed to break free of the guard's grasp, but it was no use. The Jackals were a strong breed— almost as strong as the werewolves. The guard held the prisoner's arms tightly at his sides while the other guard approached with the torture device. The jackal squeezed the man's nose until he finally opened his clenched jaw, gasping for air. The guard then seized the opportunity to thrust the tongue grippers inside. He grabbed the muscular organ and yanked until it was overextended several inches passed the man's lips. While the prisoner's screams caught in his throat, the guard wielded a razor-sharp dagger from his belt. He then sliced through the muscle until it was completely severed. Blood pooled in the prisoner's throat and blocked his airway, and his body flopped on the ground like a fish out of water. He seized for a minute before the shuddering finally stopped, and he was out of his misery.

Gortock bore his eyes into Lucian's. "So, you see now that I have ways of making people talk. Even haughty kings such as yourself have learned to bow before me." He reached down and grabbed Lucian's jaw and squeezed. "Perhaps you'd like to talk now and tell me where the Fire Opal is located."

Lucian laughed maniacally, which only irritated Gortock further. "It doesn't matter, you buffoon. You can't touch it—it won't let you get anywhere near it."

The Jackal leader kicked Lucian's hand again and grumbled, "If I can't touch it, then I bet you know who can, and I bet it's either you or one of your sons." He nodded once to his guards and stormed out of the cell. The second guard grabbed the dead prisoner by his arms and dragged the corpse out. His keys made a loud clanging sound against the cell door as he locked it.

Lucian hung his head. He wondered if he just sealed his sons' fates. Then again, he thought, by the time the Jackals found the twins, it may be too late.

Godspeed my sons.

fifteen

Damian and Logan followed the wood nymph over the crest with an intense eagerness in their steps. The closer they got to the resting place of the Fire Opal, the harder their hearts pounded.

"Where is it?" Logan growled. His impatience was bubbling to the surface, and Damian was worried his temper would explode on Valen, so he held a hand up to shush him.

Valen pointed east to a stream where there was a partially hidden cavern entrance. "It's over there in that grotto"—she looked at Damian—"It won't be easy to get, even if you are the chosen one."

"Why is that?" he asked with trepidation. Her grim expression made him feel ill at ease.

Valen's mouth was pressed in a straight line, and her eyes were filled with concern. "The legend states that it is guarded by a knight who rides a horse of fire."

"Hmm, well Logan can fight him while I fetch the opal."

"Aye," Logan yelped and grabbed his sword.

"No, he can't help you. This is your quest, and you must face the challenges alone. If he were to try, he would certainly be killed," she warned in a threatening tone.

"So, I have to go in there alone?" Damian acknowledged. "Great."

Valen lightly touched his arm. "I'll be with you. The knight won't hurt the guardian of the forest."

Damian's brow arched. "So, have you seen the sentry before?"

She gently shook her head. "No, I've never journeyed into the cavern. I'm only meant to protect its whereabouts."

"Well, if the knight won't harm you, can't you get the Fire Opal?" Logan interjected while staring at the cavern. "Also, is that the magical stream?"

She blinked rapidly at him as if something stupid just fell out of his mouth. "No, only the first son of the first son with the special mark can touch the Opal. The knight won't hurt me, but that won't protect your brother. And the stream you see is just a stream. The Fire Opal will open the Sacred Spring."

Logan's mouth opened to form a retort, but Damian quickly interrupted, "It's fine, Logan. I've got it. I'll be fine." Logan's mouth snapped shut, and he glared at the ground. "Just wait here, and I'll be back shortly."

Logan reluctantly nodded in understanding and patted Damian on the back of his shoulder before plopping down on the ground.

Valen gestured for Damian to follow her into the stream. They crossed the water, which was waist deep, to the opening of the cavern. Damian hesitated and drew several deep breaths.

"Are you ready?" she whispered.

"Aye," he replied along with one nod.

"Follow me." She ducked inside the small cavern opening, which gave way to a spacious area, and Damian followed closely behind with his hand on the hilt of his sword.

The sunlight was swallowed up by impenetrable blackness, and the only sound, aside from their stumbling steps, was that of the stream coiling around it protectively like a mother snake protecting her nest of eggs. Damian felt pebbles and rocks of other sizes through the thin souls of his wet boots as they marched forward, and it stung his feet. He was using his vampire vision to adjust to the dark, but it wasn't without difficulty. Valen clung to his arm like a small child, and it made him feel protective. If he couldn't see the knight coming, he had no idea how to fight it. He bumped into something and quickly felt it with his hands. Relieved it was just a stalagmite, he took Valen's wrist and safely wove her around it. A chilly draft whooshed around them and ruffled his hair as he pressed on. He ascertained that meant they were about to reach a juncture with another area, and he was correct. The new area had a small light in the distance, so he easily avoided the stalagmites now. There were pools of water to step around as well, and bats dove at them as they navigated their way.

"What do you think the source of light is?" he whispered.

She stood on her tiptoes to whisper into his ear, "I think it's the Fire Opal. It's called that because it's protected by a ring of fire in addition to the knight on the fiery steed."

He took her by the elbow and crept forward. When they came to the next intersection, there was a sudden loud whinny that echoed off the hollowed walls, and a burst of light. A flaming horse carrying a dark knight came charging at them, and Damian pushed Valen aside to take on the daunting force. He unsheathed his sword and wielded it in the air above his head before steadying it in front of his face. The blade felt good in his hand, and his confidence was coming back to him.

A tongue of fire shot from the horse's mouth when it cried out its anger again, and Damian had to dodge the flames. Once he recovered his footing, he swung his sword in savage fury at the shadow riding the beast of fire. The knight ducked the blade, though, and when he stared at his attacker, Damian saw his blazing eyes. Whatever the knight was, he was not going to be easy to conquer. Damian sidestepped the charging steed and jumped into the air while slicing the sword downward. This time he struck the knight, causing him to fall from his mount. The sentry regained his footing, though, and charged at Damian with his own sword carving the air.

Damian dodged the blow from the knight while wielding his own weapon. He caught flesh and fire this time, but the guard didn't fall gracefully. As the knight fell to his knees, he jabbed his weapon and sliced Damian's right side open. Warm blood spilled forth over the cold skin that was still damp from the stream, and Damian crumpled forth. He knew if he gave up now, it would be over. One more blow from his attacker would do him in.

He envisioned himself being engulfed in the knight's flaming embrace, and that gave him the extra strength he needed.

He stood and jabbed as the guard charged him, and his sword tore into flesh with a cold steel punch. The knight's body burst on impact, filling the air with a firestorm, and the horse, which had been pawing at the earth the entire time, imploded.

Damian dodged the untamed flames and used his body to shield Valen, who was crouching behind a mass of stalagmites.

"That was amazing," she whispered. "I can't believe what I just saw."

Damian laughed and nudged her arm. "You live in this crazy forest, and that is what surprises you?"

She smiled and looked away from his amused expression. "Yeah, I suppose that doesn't make a lot of sense, does it?"

He shook his head while giving her his hand to pull her up. When she took it and rose to her feet, she saw him grimace and press his shirt into his wounded abdomen.

"The spring will heal your wound," she informed him.

"We had better hurry then. I've lost a lot of blood already."

They continued walking toward the source of the light, and when they turned the corner, their mouths opened in awe—protected in an impressive ring of fire, was the magical, ruby red opal. Flames danced and reflected off its shiny surface, illuminating the cavern with a thousand dots of light. Damian approached the mystical gem with excitement bubbling in his chest. His skin prickled, and sweat ran down his face.

He glanced at Valen and smiled. "It's magnificent!" However, when he looked back at it, his face knotted. "How am I supposed to get it, though?"

"Since you are the chosen recipient, you should be able to just reach in and take it without any harm," she advised.

Damian studied the magical gem from a couple of angles. Then, with much hesitation, he reached toward it. When he felt the heat from the flames, he didn't think he was going to be able to do it, but he continued reaching past the blazes licking at his skin until he felt the heat of the Fire Opal against his palm. Without injury, he withdrew his hand and the stone. He turned it over in his palms, admiring its beauty and wondering about its magical prowess while Valen peeked around him to see it.

"Where is the spring? How do I find it?"

Valen's face went blank. "Honestly, I'm not sure. I never expected anyone to get the Fire Opal, and my predecessor must not have known either because she didn't say." She looked around the cavern. "I thought it would just appear. Maybe it's outside the cavern."

Damian looked down at the mysterious gem and ran his fingers over its smooth, glassy surface, which was still warm to the touch from the protective blaze. "Let's go outside then."

He took a couple of steps forward while clutching the opal, as if it were the most precious thing in the world, when suddenly the ground began to shake and rumble. He instinctively reached for Valen to keep her from falling while he tried to maintain his own balance.

"Do you hear that? I can hear rushing water," he exclaimed once the ground stopped trembling. He bolted around the corner to the next open area and laid his eyes on a crystal-clear spring. "There it is!" He ran to the water and fell to his knees, scooping the spring into his greedy hands to drink from it. After several gulps, he splashed some on his wound and watched in astonishment while it closed. "This is incredible! I need to go get Logan, so he can drink from it too."

"Why don't you stay here, so it doesn't close again, and I'll go fetch your brother," Valen offered.

"Okay but be careful." Damian sat by the spring and waded his hand in the cold rushing water.

Several minutes later, Logan, who was dripping wet from crossing the stream, appeared with Valen. "I don't believe it," he shouted while crouching to gain access to the water. He splashed it in his face and took hearty sips.

Logan had brought the knapsacks with him, and Damian reached for his canteen. "We need to take some to Father," he said while replacing the plain water in his container with the spring water. Logan followed suit once he was done quenching his thirst.

Damian rose to his feet and wobbled. "Whoa! I feel strange," he remarked. "I feel a peculiar energy radiating through my body. Do you feel it too, Brother?" He looked at Logan with a lopsided grin.

Logan stood and shuddered. "Aye, I do! I feel incredible." He looked at his hands, and his smile showed off his razor-sharp teeth. "I feel so much stronger!" he growled. "I want to go fight something. I want to tear into a grizzly."

Damian laughed at his twin's enthusiasm. "Save your urges for the Jackal army. Take your anger out on them."

Logan's jaw tightened in a confident smirk. "I can do both."

Damian relented with a nod. "Let's get to it then." He turned his attention to Valen. "Can you quickly guide us out of the forest?"

The wood nymph looked down at her hands and bobbed her head. "Of course I can," she said in a soft tone that was somewhat solemn. "Follow me."

"Wait"—Damian looked at the opal he still held—"I think I need to put this back where it belongs first. I don't want it to fall into anyone's hands. I want to respect its power."

Valen tilted her head while she studied the vampire. "I think that's the right thing to do. Thank you for your concern for the forest."

Damian shrugged his broad shoulders. "No big deal." He walked back to the blazing ring and placed the Fire Opal inside its protective circle. As soon as it was in place, the sound of rushing water ceased. They trotted back to where the spring had been, and it was gone. "Everything is back to normal then," Damian remarked.

A loud whinny suddenly pierced the silence, and they could hear hooves pounding on the rocky surface. "The knight is back too," Valen forewarned.

The brothers drew their swords just as the knight on his fiery steed charged around the corner. He halted the fire horse, drawing on the reins until the blazing stallion reared on its hind legs. Then the horse came clopping down on all fours, the loud sound echoing off the cavern walls. It pawed one hoof nervously while the knight stared them down with his glowing eyes. His sword was drawn and aimed at the brothers. He looked at the fire opal, then back to Damian, who was poised to battle again.

"I respect what you do here," Damian announced, "The opal is back where it belongs, and we are leaving." The knight looked at the Fire Opal again and then turned to Damian to give him a nod while sheathing his sword. He nudged the horse and trotted out of sight.

"Let's get out of here," Logan blurted. "Let's get out of this creepy-ass forest."

Damian shook his head in agreement and led them back to the cave entrance. "Which way?" he asked Valen while looking around the surrounding terrain.

Her eyes were full of remorse when she pointed northeast. "We need to go this way. It should be a short journey."

Damian studied the wood nymph as they climbed the hill protecting the cavern. He'd noticed her sadness and wondered if it was because she was lonely in the forest, or if it was something more. He felt a growing fondness for her and wondered if she felt it too. *If so, is it for me or Logan?*

Damian looked up at the sky. There was only a handful of daylight left, so the twins needed to make haste. They didn't want to have to navigate their way out of the eerie forest at night.

"Will it take long to reach the edge of the woodland?" he asked her.

Valen met his eyes, and the corner of her lip turned down. "No, it shouldn't."

"Good," Logan grumbled. "I'm anxious to get to the Jackal's lair and fight." The surge of power he was feeling from the Sacred Spring amazed him. It was balling up inside him, burning like the sun, and he needed to direct it at something.

Feeling his brother's restlessness, Damian commented, "All in good time, Brother. We'll get there soon."

They walked in silence and without incident until, suddenly, a vine snaked out and grabbed Damian by his wrist. It flung him into a tree and began to tightly bind him. It lashed around him, growing tighter with every whip, and began to squeeze the life out of him like a giant boa constrictor. Logan rushed with his sword in hand, but before the first strike, the vine suddenly ruptured into hundreds of chunks as Damian broke free with his new-found strength. He took in deep gulps of the murky air with his hands on his pained chest.

"That was interesting," he mumbled in between gasps.

"How in the hell did you do that?" Logan was baffled and stared at him with scrutiny.

Damian shook his head once and opened his arms in demonstration. "I just pushed my arms out."

"Huh. You were strong, but not that strong," his brother observed, "It has to be the spring water."

"I agree. I feel capable of anything." Damian strutted in front of Valen and Logan. "I feel completely ready to take on the Jackal clan."

"We're close to the edge of the forest now," Valen announced after they'd walked a little farther. "It's about two hundred feet yet, and then we'll be there." She pointed ahead of them.

Damian was excited about being closer to saving his father, and he was relieved to get out of the dangerous forest; however, he felt a pang of sadness about leaving the nymph.

Sixteen

As soon as they reached the break in the trees, Logan announced, "I'm going hunting." He didn't hesitate to strip in front of Valen without any shame. He shifted and bounded off through the open terrain while the nymph stared with her mouth gaping.

"I apologize for my brother," Damian muttered with reddened cheeks. "I think he should be more respectful about the company he's in."

"Oh, I suppose it's the nature of the beast," she replied with a blush of her own. "And speaking of which, what about you? You'll need to feed as well," she gently reminded him.

Damian looked away from her searching stare. He didn't like being what he was in front of her—it made him feel ashamed. "I'll worry about that later. I care more about getting to Father."

Valen tilted her head, and a touch of admiration pooled in her haunting violet eyes. "Your love for your father makes you seem more human than vampire, which brings about another question if you don't mind me asking. How are you a vampire? Was your mother one?"

Damian's lip twitched, and his eyes fell to the ground at the mention of his dead mother. He drew a deep shuddering breath and then went on to explain his unusual family dynamic. "My mother was human, but Logan and I both took after our father. However, a clan of vampires abducted me when we were two"—his face contorted as his mind took him back to the event—"They made me drink their blood, and they drank mine; it was necessary for the conversion. Then they brought a young girl to me, who wasn't much older than I was, and made me bite her. I can still recall with almost perfect clarity how her big blue eyes had glassed over while I claimed her life."

Valen's gasp interrupted him. "Asking a child to kill a child is just horrible."

He nodded in shame. "It was, but what they would've done to her would've been so much worse. I actually did her a favor."

She shuddered from the mental image he planted. "How did you get away? Did your father save you?"

Pride shone in Damian's smile. "Aye, he and his knights attacked and wiped out nearly all the vampires"—his face fell as he continued—"but it was too late for me. The conversion was complete by then."

Valen paced in small circles, clinging to every word he spoke. "So, you are still werewolf too, are you not? Do you still feel its influence?"

"No, I just feel the pull of the vampire. Sometimes, I wish I could feel the wolf, just so I could be closer to my family," he somberly replied. "I often feel disconnected from my father and my twin."

Valen looked over her shoulder back at the Hoia-Baciu Forest and sighed. "I wonder if it has changed, though."

"What do you mean? If what has changed?"

She stopped pacing and turned to face him. "Well, you drank from the Sacred Spring, and it heals"—she pointed to his abdomen—"Just like it healed your stomach, maybe it healed that part of you too. Maybe it has restored your true nature."

Damian's eyes went wide. "Do you think so? I feel different—that's true enough—but I don't know that I've reconnected with the wolf. I was too young when the change took place to remember what the beast feels like."

Her eyes lit up and were as bright as the smile she wore. "Wouldn't it be amazing, though?"

He dragged his hand across his chin, feeling his stubble growth scrape his fingers and palm. "Aye, that would be something unexpected." His head turned to his left when he overheard whistling in the distance. Logan had returned, and he looked satiated. He was still licking his lips.

"What?" he asked Damian when he noticed his brother's scowl.

"Have you no shame?" Damian gestured to the man's naked form.

Logan glanced at Valen, who was looking away from them, and replied, "I suppose I don't. If it pleases you to look, wood nymph, then by all means look."

A blush crept up her cheeks again, causing an eruption of laughter from the werewolf.

"Logan, act like a prince, not an animal," Damian growled at his brother.

"But I am an animal," he sang out and howled before reaching for his clothes.

Damian turned his back to him and took hold of Valen's arm. "Let me apologize once more for him, and let me thank you again for your help."

She looked up into his face, shielding her eyes from the bright sun, and softly mewed, "You're welcome."

"Let's go, Brother," Logan exclaimed.

Damian let go of her arm and waved good-bye. As he walked away with his twin, though, she called out to him.

"Stop! I want to go with you," she announced.

Damian's eyes widened, and he studied her anxious expression. "What's that you say?"

"I said I want to go with you. I want to help," she offered.

Logan's hearty laughter filled the air. "Battle is no place for a woman, and you'll just slow us down."

Valen lifted her chin haughtily. "I seem to recall you doubting my strength when we first met, and you ended up on your back."

Damian remembered it too, and he doubled over with laughter. "She's right. You did end up on your ass." Then his expression turned serious, and he addressed Valen. "But he's correct that battle isn't a place for a woman—even a woman with your skills."

She scowled at his words. "I'm not a woman, I'm a guardian, and that makes me a warrior too. You can either let me travel with you, or I can follow you there, but I'm going."

Damian looked down at the grass and frowned. He saw this turning into a time-consuming argument, and he didn't need that. "I don't understand why you want to come with us," he mumbled.

"I want to go with you because your fight is for a noble cause, and if you do rescue your father, maybe he can take the Hoia-Baciu Forest as part of his lands and issue a protective order to keep travelers out of it"—her expression grew soft—"I also want to go because I'm lonely. I want to experience life outside of the forest for once."

Logan pointed to the woodland. "It seems to me that this crazy forest does okay in protecting itself from wanderers."

She looked back at her home. "Yes, it does protect itself, but there's something you don't know. It's growing—every time it must defend itself, it grows stronger and vaster. It's not a significant growth that can easily be seen, but I've kept track. It's already widened a quarter of a mile in the past seven years."

The brothers exchanged a wide-eyed glance. "Interesting," Damian stated, "We could speak to our father on your behalf then."

She crossed her arms defiantly. "I can speak to him myself."

Damian ran his hands through his hair and let out a heavy sigh. "I can see your mind is made up. If you're determined to come along and fight, though, you should take a drink of the spring water." He thrust the canteen in her direction.

She held her hand up in refusal, though. "Wood nymphs aren't meant to be immortal. When we die, our bodies begin a new forest. We are part of the earth—I belong to it, and I can't mess with that design."

"Suit yourself. Let's go," Logan scoffed, and Damian nodded in agreement but stood still, looking at the open land in front of them.

"I wonder which way we should go," he stated while fondling the hilt of his dagger. "When Father banished them, where did they retreat to, and are they still there?"

"They aren't within five miles of here because that's how far I hunted," Logan answered.

"I say we go toward the Mures River and look for them there. Maybe we'll come across a village, and they'll know where to look. That will also give you a chance to feed, Brother."

"Aye," Damian agreed. He needed to feed soon. He longed for the taste of blood again.

Seventeen

King Lucian stared at his throbbing hand, but it wasn't the painful swelling that his mind was focused on. He was seeing his sons in his mind's eye and wondering where they were in their journey. He was worried they got into trouble within the Haunted Forest. Would they even know to go there for the Fire Opal to open the Sacred Spring? His wife had visited him in his dreams and told him that they were on their way, and that she had led them to the forest, but it was just a dream after all. *Wasn't it?* It had seemed quite real, so maybe it was her spirit contacting him. His sons were smart, though, and hopefully humble enough to know that they wouldn't be able to defeat the Jackal clan without drinking from the magical spring.

His cell door clanged and groaned as a guard swung it open and stepped inside with Gortock right behind him. "Good morning, Lucian. How is my guest feeling today?" the leader asked with sarcasm. "Are you ready to have that talk, or do you need more convincing?"

The weary king looked at his captor under hooded eyes. "I don't know what you expect from me. I've already told you that you can't touch the Fire Opal," he seethed, "so you might as well give up on that idea."

The sadistic jackal laughed. "You werewolves have always been such a stubborn lot,

so full of pride. I don't need to touch the Opal—
I'll have your sons do all the work for me. I just
need the spring revealed"—he clasped his paws
and rubbed—"and then I'll kill them both, or
maybe I'll enslave them instead. Now that is a
fantastic idea, don't you think?"

Lucian knew the jackal wanted him to
break down and plead for their lives, but he wasn't
going to give him the satisfaction. "I think you're
too late," he smugly replied.

Gortock's grim smile sent an undeniable
shiver through Lucian's body. "Let's see how
cooperative you decide to be after some time in the
coffin"—he turned to his guard and waved his
paw—"String him up."

Lucian knew of the torture device Gortock
had in mind for him. He would be stripped naked,
put inside the confining metal cage, and hung from
the gallows on public display. Onlookers would leer
at him and most likely poke him with sharp objects.
Some would throw rocks or rotten food at him. It
would be humiliating for sure, but he would cope
if it meant protecting his sons. He had to hold onto
hope that they were near.

EIGHTEEN

The odd trio trekked across the open plain toward the Mures River in silence. Damian kept throwing glances at Valen, though. He couldn't figure the nymph out. He wondered why she would risk her life to help them, and he wondered if she would be able to help at all. He would need to rescue his father and give him a sip of the spring water before he could focus his attention on her, and by then it may be too late. She accepted her mortality as part of nature's cycle, but he didn't want to see her die.

"You look anxious," she suddenly said. "The lines are deep on your forehead."

Glancing down at her, he replied, "I am anxious. You do realize that I can't look after you until after we've rescued Father, don't you? I must first get to him and give him spring water, and that will leave you vulnerable."

"I know," she softly answered and placed her delicate hand on the hilt of her small sword, "and I can look after myself just fine. I'm going along to help, not to be in your way."

Damian's chest expanded with a heavy sigh, and he explained his other fear. "There's something else worrying me too. Gortock is renowned for his sadistic torture methods. He shows no mercy to those he considers his enemy."

Her face fell, and she quietly told him, "Well, I can see your cause for alarm then."

Logan had overheard the conversation, and he was clenching his fists tight enough to turn his large knuckles white. "They'd better not have tried anything on Father," he growled. Then he looked down at Valen and asked, "Does that change your mind about coming? It's not too late for you to go back."

She shook her head defiantly, though. "No, it doesn't, and I imagine that the king of werewolves is strong enough to handle whatever they do to him."

Damian looked to the sky and mumbled, "God, I hope so." He shook his head, trying to void out the mental images of his father being tortured by Gortock.

"I say we use their methods on them when we take them prisoner—an eye for an eye," Logan exclaimed with a wicked smile.

"I don't know about that because it takes too much time. I think we should just save Father and then destroy them all," Damian responded with authority.

Valen grabbed his arm and pointed southwest. "Look, there's smoke."

"Great," he said, and his smile showed off his fangs. "There must be a village there. We can stop and ask for directions and get something to eat." He saw her cringe out of the corner of his eye and felt the need to apologize for being what he was. "I'm sorry, but I'm famished. As you said about my brother, it's the nature of the beast."

She shrugged her small shoulders. "I know, but that doesn't mean I have to like it. However, I'm all about protecting the forest, not humans, so do what you must."

Logan patted his chiseled stomach. "I could eat again as well, and I smell something roasting."

Damian sniffed the air, and he realized he could also smell roasting hog, which was unusual for him. His sense of smell wasn't nearly as keen as Logan's, especially when it pertained to animal flesh. Maybe Valen is correct, and the wolf is waking up inside me.

nineteen

It was dusk when they found a tiny village, which was comprised of only four huts. The fire in the center of the shacks was still smoldering, and there was a small portion of hog on the spit yet. Logan quickly snatched the remaining pork up and devoured it in two large bites.

"Logan! Maybe our companion would've liked some," Damian scolded.

Logan gave a sheepish grin and licked his chops clean, not looking the least bit sorry.

"No, it's all right. I live off nourishment from the flowers and trees, and I can find some berries in the woods," she said softly so as not to alert the villagers of their presence.

Logan paced around the bonfire. "Speaking of nourishment, don't you need to feed, Brother?"

Damian took in a deep breath, searching the air for the scent of female blood, but it was lacking. "No," he snarled, "nothing here appeals to me. Besides, we need information first. We should knock on some doors."

"I have an easier way to get their attention," Logan replied with a big grin before howling at the top of his lungs. Four doors opened at once, and men bearing firearms emerged from each. The guns were quickly aimed at the brothers and Valen.

A big burly man roared, "Who goes there?" His gun was steadied on Logan.

Damian held one hand up in peace. "We mean you no harm. We are merely travelers in search of the Jackal tribe. Please provide us with directions to their camp."

A small man eased his gun down with a chuckle. "That's it? You only want directions?" He looked at the others, waiting for them to lower their weapons as well, but they didn't.

Damian gave the slight man a nod. "Aye, that's all we are looking for. Do you know of the Jackal clan?"

The burly man was the one who responded this time. "We know of them indeed. Are you looking to band with them?"

Logan quickly growled, "No! We are going to slaughter every last one of them!" He took a threatening step toward the man. "Do you pledge your allegiance to the scoundrels?"

The muscular man cocked his weapon. "If I were you, I'd back up," he threatened with a deep scowl.

Logan laughed in response and held his ground, though.

"It's all right. My brother told you that we mean you no harm, and his word is good. Besides, you can't hurt us," he explained, "we are immortals."

The large man scrunched his brows together. "Really? Well, if you keep approaching me, I'll be testing that theory out."

Logan took another step toward him with his arms wide open, and just as he promised, he fired the weapon into Logan's stomach. Logan smiled a wide toothy grin and brushed his fingers over the wound as if it was dirt he was wiping away.

While the men stared in awe, the wound healed itself.

The small man leapt backward and yowled, "Jumping jackrabbits! How did you do that?"

Logan laughed and shrugged his massive shoulders. "I just told you, you fool, that we are immortal," he stated with a smug smile. "Now, as you can see, you should put those guns away and have a talk with us." He narrowed his eyes on the burly man. "Before you make us angry."

"Enough, Logan," Damian chastised. "You didn't answer my brother before. Do you pledge your loyalty to the Jackals?"

Another man, with pale hair, answered for the men while gesturing to the expanse of their small camp. "Look around you. This was once a large, thriving village. Then the Jackal clan came down on us like a firestorm from hell, killing everyone but us. We had escaped with our lives, but our women and children paid the price for it. So, no, we pledge nothing to the beasts. We damn them to hell!"

The others expressed their agreement by raising their guns into the air.

Damian was intrigued. "When was this?"

The men filed to the fire and sat down. The largest man stoked the smoldering embers with an iron poker before looking back at the twins. His voice was thick with remorse and hatred swirled together. "This was a year ago at least. They burned our village and killed almost everyone. Some unfortunate souls were dragged away as prisoners. I imagine they, too, are now dead. For their sakes, I hope so." A tear escaped his eye, and his body shuddered. "What did they do to you?"

Logan replied before Damian could. "The bastards killed our mother, along with the staff, and abducted our father, King Lucian Dragovich."

"I've heard of Lucian Dragovich. He's the son of King Titus, who was known to be a fair and just leader, but I thought his kingdom was destroyed."

Damian sucked in his lower lip, revealing his fangs. "That's a tale for another day. The point is, we are looking for their camp, so we can rescue our father and seek our revenge. Do you know where they went from here? Where do they hide?"

The man shook his head solemnly. "No, not for certain. We heard rumors, though, that they headed northwest toward Budapest, but we can't prove it to be true. Now, let me introduce myself. I am Dar, and these are my friends, Oliver, Liam, and Rutger. What are your names?"

"I am Damian Dragovich, and he is my twin brother, Logan," he answered while pointing in Logan's direction. Then his voice softened slightly, and he nodded toward Valen. "She is Valen—a wood nymph from the Hoia-Baciu Forest."

A gasp collectively settled over the men, and they jumped backward away from her. Oliver, the smaller man, stammered, "The-the Haunted Forest?" They all stared at the nymph in disbelief that such a fragile looking creature could survive in such a disturbing place.

She gave a soft smile to ease them. "That's right. It's my home, and I guard it."

Liam, the pale blond, replied, "Well, if you are its guardian, then what are you doing with them?"

Damian responded for her. "It's a long story, but she wants to fight with us."

"A female who wants to battle the Jackal clan?" Dar exclaimed. "I cannot fathom such a thing."

The other men were just as dumbfounded.

"I have my reasons, and don't underestimate me," she defended herself. "I'm a practiced warrior."

Rutger, who had been silent to that point, whispered to the others, "Can we talk over there?" He nodded toward the shadows by one of the huts. They each stood and silently followed the man.

Damian listened to them, despite the fact that they spoke in hushed tones. They were questioning whether or not to offer their assistance in the battle against the Jackal clan. "He thinks they should come with us," he told Logan and Valen. "What do you think, Brother?"

Logan rubbed the stubble on his chin. "Well, we're letting her come along, so why not? They may actually be able to help us make quick work of the army. Perhaps, though, we should share some of the spring water with them. We do have two canteens full, so we could let them share one and keep the other for Father."

Damian nodded in agreement with his brother, but Valen objected. "The spring water isn't meant for human beings any more than it's meant for wood nymphs. There is a balance to life and death that must be respected."

"Then we are just leading them to slaughter," Damian argued, "and I don't want to be responsible for that. I say if they decide to come along, they should take a sip for protection."

"Aye, I agree," Logan grumbled. "They won't be of use to us without it. They'd just be another distraction."

Valen looked away from the young werewolf's scrutinizing stare. She knew he was referring to her. "Well, I suppose I'm outnumbered then," she quietly relented.

The four men returned just then and took their seats around the fire. "We would like to go with you," Dar said with conviction. "We would like the chance to finally seek our revenge."

"We know," Damian replied. "We overheard you talking. You are brave to want to go up against the Jackal clan, but foolishly so."

Dar shrugged and replied, "Perhaps so, but what do we have to lose? The bastards have taken everything from us. Our deaths won't be in vain as long as we kill at least one of the creatures."

Damian nodded in understanding and admired their courage. "Well, we have a way to ensure your victory and longevity of life as well," he proclaimed.

Four heads snapped in his direction with expressions of intrigue. "How so?" Dar inquired on their behalf.

Damian held up his canteen. "We have water from the Sacred Spring—it's how we became fully immortal. You are invited and encouraged to take a drink to protect yourselves." He thrusted the canteen to Liam, who sat the closest. The man looked at the container with hesitation, though.

"Go ahead," Logan encouraged him in a gruff voice. "It's not poison."

A blush crept into the blond's pale cheeks. "I believe you. It's just that I don't know if I want to live forever without my Sara and my young lad,

William. This past year has been difficult enough, so I can't fathom endless years to come."

"Oh, I see," Damian replied with an empathetic pat on the man's shoulder. He thrusted the canteen to Dar, who was standing on the other side of Liam. "How about you then? Would you like immortal life?"

Dar reached for the water, but he hesitated midway before taking hold of the container with his large hands. "Aye, I would like to live to see another day"—he glanced at his friends with a big smile while he unscrewed the cap—"or two." He pressed the nozzle to his lips and took a healthy gulp before passing it along to Rutger. The quiet man eagerly accepted the canteen and took a swig. He tried to hand it off to Oliver, but the smaller man shook his head. "No, I agree with Liam. It's been too hard to face the days without my beloved Hilda, but I thank you for the offer, and I'll fight with everything in me until I draw my last breath."

Rutger handed the canteen back to Damian, who accepted it with a shrug. "Well, you have time to change your minds." He looked up at the blackened sky. "We will wait until dawn to begin our journey since you lack the night vision we have. I suggest you get some rest while Logan and I protect the camp." One by one, the men filed back inside their huts while Damian, Logan, and Valen sat in front of the fire. "Valen, you should sleep too," he suggested softly. The wood nymph simply nodded and lay down on the hard ground. It only took a minute for her soft snores to fill the air.

"Are you tired, Damian?" Logan asked in what he probably considered to be a whisper. Valen stirred some, so Damian put his finger to his lips.

"No, I feel just as energized as I did earlier. It must be the spring water," he whispered.

"I do too," Logan replied in a softer voice this time. "I'm going to go hunting. I'm famished." He shed his clothes, transformed, and bounded into the woods nearby.

Damian dug inside his knapsack for what little bit of salt pork he had left and made quick work of it, noticing that the taste was off. The difference wasn't huge, but it was noticeable. He shrugged it off and dug through the sack for the rabbit pelt, which he folded in half and slipped underneath Valen's head. He wasn't sure what came over him, but he planted a soft kiss on her temple and sat back on his haunches to watch her sleep.

Women had been objects to him—they were for satiating his hunger for blood and lust. However, Valen wasn't a woman. She was a wood nymph and new rules applied.

TWENTY

Since neither of them could sleep, the night was a long one for Damian and Logan. They mostly discussed what they had planned for the Jackal clan. Damian kept a watchful eye on Valen while she slept—he didn't want her to fall prey to any of the men in the tiny village. He clenched his fists in jealousy at the mere thought of it. She roused as soon as the sun peeked over the horizon and found him staring at her. A look of surprise crossed her delicate features, and she jumped backward.

"Did I startle you?" he asked in a playful tone.

Her cheeks turned a pale pink, and she looked away from his deep gaze. "Yes, I'm not used to waking up to others. I forgot where I was at first," she explained while looking around at the silent huts.

His eyes crinkled with amusement. "I suppose it is different for you after living alone in the Haunted Forest."

"I should say so," she whispered more to herself than to him.

"Are you glad to be away from there, though? I mean, it must be a pleasant break to be away from such a dreadful place," he wondered.

She looked all around herself before telling him, "It's different out here, but I don't see the Hoia-Baciu Forest the way you do. It isn't a frightening place to me—it's my home"—she brushed a stray lock of hair back and stared into his searching eyes—"However, it does get lonely there, so I find your company to be a welcomed change."

Damian smiled, and she could see his sharp fangs.

"I enjoy your company as well, but what about other wood nymphs? Why are you alone when another could be there with you?"

She shrugged her small shoulders, and her lip pulled down. "I'm not sure how it happened, but our numbers have dwindled. Therefore, we have to stay spread out to protect the various woodlands." A breeze blew past and made her shiver, so Damian stoked the fire, which had diminished to just a flicker.

"Here, wrap this around your shoulders," he said while picking up the rabbit pelt she'd slept on. While she donned the warm covering, he put kindling from a nearby stack onto the fire and worked it into a full-blown blaze. "There. That should help some."

Valen patted the pelt and asked, "Don't you need this? Aren't you cold too?"

Damian waved her off. "I'm okay. You need it more than I do." He ran his hand over his bare arm, and his brows came together. "Now that you mention it, I don't really feel that cold at all. I suppose maybe it's from the spring water." The last part came out more as a question than a statement.

She tilted her head in thought. "I'm not sure, but since it has medicinal properties, I guess that could be true." The sound of rustling made her look over his shoulder. Damian didn't have to look, though, to know that it was just Logan—he could smell the fresh blood on his brother's breath.

"I'm full now, Brother. I found a huge black bear, and it really hit the spot," Logan mused while rubbing his stomach for effect. "Now, we should probably make use of the Mures River before we begin our journey to Budapest."

Damian's lip twitched. "I agree. You're starting to smell a little gamey."

Logan scowled at his brother. "And here I thought I smelled like roses. Let's go." He pointed to Valen. "Will you wake up our guests while we bathe?"

She looked down at her delicate hands, which were resting in her lap, and murmured, "I'd actually like to have the opportunity to cleanse as well. I'd wait until you are finished, but since we are pressed for time, I think I should do it now."

"Good morning, my new friends," Dar's voice suddenly boomed and made them all look in his direction. "I trust you are ready to get started, so I'll wake the others."

"There. That solves that problem," Valen said as she rose to her feet and began the short hike to the river.

"We're going to bathe, and then we can go," Damian announced to Dar before trotting to catch up to the wood nymph. Logan was close behind him, and they found Valen at the river's edge. She was stripping her clothing off without modesty. Damian's voice caught in his throat when he told her, "Um, we'll go farther down to give you your privacy."

She looked up at him and lightly laughed. "If I'm not afraid to die in front of you, then I think I shouldn't be afraid for you to see me as I am," she proclaimed and stood naked for his greedy gaze.

Damian tried to look away, but he shamefully stared. She had such a delicate body. Her small breasts were thrust forward and topped with blushing pink tips, her hips were slightly flared beneath a trim waist, and the hair covering her apex looked soft to the touch. When she turned away to enter the water, he got an eyeful of her small, round bottom, and he desperately wanted to pat it. He was already rock-hard with a pulsing heat that begged for release. He quickly glanced at Logan to make sure his brother wouldn't do something out of line, but the werewolf was already splashing around in the chilly water. Damian stripped naked and plunged in near him, but it wasn't before his brother caught a glimpse of his excitement and howled with laughter.

"She does it for you, huh?" he asked with a chuckle. Damian only responded with a scowl, so Logan continued his taunting, "Go get it then."

"Would you please quit?" Damian seethed through clenched teeth.

Logan held his hands up in defense and backed away to finish his bathing. Damian allowed himself a quick glance in Valen's direction and found her watching him with a quirky smile. He dropped his gaze and washed himself while letting the frigid water put his shaft back to a normal state. He watched her, though, when she bounded out of the swirling river and redressed herself. She looked so innocent, and he couldn't help but want to tarnish her.

He and Logan followed her back to the camp shortly afterward and found all the men sitting around the fire talking to her. The aroma of pork once again filled the air while Oliver turned the spit. Liam noticed the brothers before the others and waved his hand at them.

"Welcome back," he cheerfully greeted them. "You're just in time to have breakfast with us."

Damian was hungry for blood, but the roasted hog would have to do for now. There would be more villages on the way to Budapest.

Logan was already sitting down. "Good. I could eat again."

"We'll eat quickly and then start our travels," Damian announced to the group. He took his place next to Valen, who was munching on some leaves and flowers. "Do you feel refreshed?"

She looked up from her makeshift feast and mumbled with a full mouth, "Yes, I feel better."

The members of the crude group enjoyed their meal together, speculating on their journey and how long it would take. The consensus was that it would take a few days if they didn't waste any daylight. When they finished eating, they packed up the remaining meat along with their weapons and began the long trek northwest.

TWENTY-ONE

They chose to travel alongside the Mures River, so they'd have water for drinking, cooking, and bathing. Also, they'd have more luck in finding villages where they could gather information about the Jackal clan. Damian was hopeful he'd also find women in the villages. He didn't feel weak, but he longed for the taste of blood.

By nightfall, just a few miles inside the woodlands, they arrived at the village of Arad. They weren't welcomed, though, until they had a chance to explain their mission.

The village elder, Mikael, explained, "Outsiders usually take from us. They steal our supplies and our animals, but if you are truly after the Jackal clan, then you are welcomed to anything you need. Some of the young men may even go with you to fight—there's safety in numbers."

Damian glanced at his canteen of spring water and scowled. He didn't have enough water to protect any of the villagers. There was only a small amount left that he was saving in case Oliver or Liam changed their minds, and Logan's container was for their father.

"I'm afraid it would be too dangerous for your men," he mumbled. "It would be a suicide mission."

Mikael tugged on his white goatee with a withered hand. "You have a woman traveling with you, and you're worried about the Arad men? Or, do you just have her along to prepare your meals and empty your balls?"

Had Mikael been younger, Damian would've punched him hard in the jaw for defiling Valen through his words. Instead, he growled, "I'll ask that you only speak respectfully about her. She has personal reasons for going into battle with us, and she is a skilled warrior among her kind."

Another man of advanced years approached Mikael with a somber expression. "It won't be much longer, my friend. She's almost gone."

Mikael clasped the man's shoulder and told him, "Well, she lived a good life, Tomas. She had many good years upon this earth."

Damian had the solution to his dilemma— he'd be the Angel of Death once more, and no one would be the wiser. He'd make her transition a peaceful and quick one. He'd end her suffering.

"The Jackals have let Arad be for now," a man named Kristoff told Damian and the others while they supped with the villagers. "But some of us have been victims to their attacks on other villages—villages we once called home." A single tear trickled down the man's dirty cheek, and Damian surmised the man had lost loved ones in one of their attacks. "As long as they live, no one is safe from Gortock's wrath"—he wiped the tear away with the back of his hand and stared hard into Damian's eyes—"I'm too old to fight, but I know there are men who want to battle alongside you."

Cheers went up among the group as the men yelled in agreement with Kristoff. Damian looked at his brother, who simply shrugged, and swiped his massive hand over his face. "It's a dangerous journey your men are volunteering for, but I suppose we can't stop them if their minds are set on it."

Logan stood up and announced, "Just don't expect us to be watching over you. We'll be busy rescuing our father and taking the Jackals' heads"—he nudged Damian's shoulder to get his attention—"I'm going to go hunt. I won't go far."

"Hunt at night? Why? You just ate," Mikael stated.

Logan smiled a toothy grin at the elder. "I need fresh blood, though, and the thrill of the kill calms the beast."

"Beast? Who are you?" a plump woman asked with a condemning stare.

Damian could almost read his brother's thoughts. He knew that Logan would transform on the spot just to shock the group, so he gave him a firm disapproving glare. Logan rolled his eyes at his twin and heaved a heavy sigh.

"They're going to find out soon enough anyway," he remarked.

"Find out what?" a stocky man questioned while noticeably backing up some.

"Yeah, what is it we're supposed to know?" another seconded.

"I'll be obliged to show you," Logan claimed with a smirk and tugged on his shirt to pull it over his head.

"Logan! Show some discretion," Damian chastised him in a booming voice.

Logan's face fell, but he looked around for a spot hidden by the shadows of the night. Once the darkness concealed him, he finished undressing and transformed into the aberration. His howl pierced the frigid air, scattering the nearby birds and making the villagers leap to their feet.

"What in God's name was that?" a woman bellowed with the color drained from her round face.

"It's the devil coming for us," another exclaimed.

The men had their weapons drawn and were searching the darkness for any sign of movement. Even the elder had a dagger poised in his right hand.

"It's the Jackals. They know of our plans and have come to punish us," Mikael proclaimed.

Everyone was talking at once, so Damian loudly cleared his throat to gain their attention. "It's none of those things; it's just Logan."

On cue, Logan stepped forward with fur sprouted all over his massive form. He swiped the air with clawed hands, and saliva dripped from his razor-sharp fangs when he snarled at the group.

The men appeared ready to advance with their weapons wielded in the air, so Damian stepped in front, blocking their path. "He won't hurt you," he assured the frightened group. "He's just showing off." He turned to Logan and reprimanded him, "Go hunt and then compose yourself again."

Logan leapt past the onlookers and bounded into the thick forest.

The men turned on Damian and eyed him suspiciously. "What are you? Do you turn into that awful creature too?" Kristoff inquired with his weapon still held out in front of him.

Damian shook his head and motioned to the campfire. "Sit down by the fire, and I shall regale you with stories about the kingdom of Drago."

***

After Logan had returned and the villagers were fast asleep, Damian found the terminally ill woman. She was bundled under a pile of blankets, which he carefully peeled back. He pushed the sleeve of her nightgown up, disturbing her slumber, and her eyes flew open. She opened her small, wrinkled mouth to scream, but he quickly covered it with a meaty hand.

"Shh," he cautioned. "I'm here to help you. I'm here to give you a peaceful death." He bit into her arm to let her blood flow freely into his mouth, and he suckled until he heard her last heartbeat. The nectar had a foul taste that didn't sit well with him. He wasn't sure if it had to do with her illness or her age, but the flavor was off. Of course, there would be more villages along their journey to Budapest, so he'd have another chance to quench his thirst. He slunk out of the cabin and back toward the fire where his brother waited. Valen was asleep on the ground, so he approached with quiet steps. He gently tucked the blanket she'd been given around her form and stroked a lock of hair out of her face. Finally feeling fatigued, he lay down beside her and drifted off.

TWENTY-TWO

Dawn's first light brought about muffled cries from the cabin Damian had visited the night before. Tomas emerged from the tiny cottage with his wife draped across his frail arms, tears streaming down his wrinkled face.

"It's over now. She's at peace," he said through his sobs.

"I'm sorry, Tomas," Mikael comforted him, "but she's better off now. Jon can help you bury her."

Tomas lay her body on the ground, and her sleeve pushed upward, exposing her arm and the bite mark. His head snapped up to shoot a glare at Damian. "You? You drank from her?" He turned his aggression to Mikael. "I knew we should've made them leave! You said we'd be safe," he roared.

Damian calmly defended himself, "It's not like you think. I helped her transition to the other side in a peaceful manner. She didn't hurt." He noticed Valen listening in, so he felt the need to add, "I did her a favor. I showed her compassion where she saw prolonged agony. I gave her release from her suffering."

Tomas stroked his dead wife's hair. "You make it sound so simple, so casual and natural. Your existence is full of ugliness. You prey on helpless victims to appease your appetite with no regard for human life."

"That was not the case here. You'd have her cling to desperation despite the pain she was clearly in. You'd have her suffering prolonged if it meant you'd have more time with her, but that isn't right. It wasn't fair to her. If I meant harm to anyone, I would've chosen another—perhaps a young maiden—to satisfy my hunger."

Mikael patted the grieving man on his shoulder. "I think the young vampire is right, Tomas. She's better off this way. You know the pain she had to endure."

Tomas looked at his motionless wife and broke down. "I've been a selfish old fool! She was holding on for me—she clung to life for me." His eyes, pooled with tears, looked up to meet Damian's. "I suppose I should thank you for putting her out of her misery then."

Damian felt sorry for the man. As a vampire, it was difficult for him to maintain compassion for humans because they were his prey, but he truly felt empathy for this man. Perhaps, he thought, it was because he was grieving the loss of his mother.

Logan burst through the woods then at breakneck speed. "Damian, I spotted a Jackal hunting party," he hollered on a pant.

"The Jackals! Why would they be near here? What are they after?" Mikael yelped. "They've come to smite us!"

The village men rushed to gather weapons and hide their wives and children, while Dar and the others prepared for the attack.

"They're looking for us," Damian seethed through clenched teeth.

"What do we do? Do we just sit and wait for them to attack us?" Dar asked, gripping his pistol so hard that his knuckles turned white.

Damian exchanged a knowing glance with his twin. "We think that we'd be better off if we advance on them. They won't be expecting that," he stated on his and Logan's behalf. "Those of us who drank the spring water can be in front for the first strike."

"Spring water?" Tomas asked. "What are you talking about?"

Damian didn't want to get trapped in that conversation, but Dar quickly replied, "We drank water from something called the Sacred Spring. Allegedly, it grants us immortal life."

The older man waved him off and grumbled, "Pfftt. This life isn't something I'd want to cling to, and I ain't ever heard of such a thing."

Dar wiped his hand through his matted hair. "Well, we'll find out soon enough if it's real or not."

Others caught up to them then, wielding all types of sharp weapons from pitchforks to daggers. Only a few had pistols. They each looked to Damian and Logan for direction.

"We're ready," the man named Jon claimed while thrusting his dagger into the air.

"They're coming from the northwest section of the woods," Logan informed them. "There were at least fifteen that I counted, but that could just be the first wave of the battalion."

"No," Damian grunted and shook his head. "Gortock wouldn't leave himself and his fortress unprotected. It's probably just a small hunting party. I imagine he's cocky enough to think that it would only take that number of soldiers to eliminate us."

Logan scuffed his booted foot on the ground and popped his thick neck. "You're probably right, but we should still be prepared to be greatly outnumbered."

"Of course, my brother, but don't forget we have the powers of the Sacred Spring on our side."

"You also have me," Valen quietly mentioned, creeping up behind Damian to stand at his side. "And before you object, think of this as an opportunity to see how well I handle myself in battle."

Damian's jaw clenched tightly. He wasn't ready to see her in danger, and he didn't think he ever would be. "If you insist," he acquiesced with a sigh.

"When do we leave?" Oliver asked with his loaded gun in hand.

"They'll be closing in on us soon, so we should go now," Logan suggested and drew his sword.

"Is there anything we should know about them?" Rutger asked.

Damian slowly nodded. "Yes, they're quick, and they're ruthless"—he stopped and sniffed the air—"And they're just over that hill," he said and pointed west.

TWENTY-
THREE

Lucian felt a sharp sting in his back and tried to turn his head to see what had imposed it, but his confines were too tight for him to move at all. He'd been dangling in the torture coffin for a few days now and had been deprived of food and water, apart from what had been thrown at him. His head wouldn't even be upright if it weren't for the coffin's design. The fallen king presumed it would be only another day or two before he gave in to the blackness of death. Another sharp blow to his back made his eyes roll. This time, peals of laughter followed the infliction.

"It won't be long now," Gortock sneered. "Honestly, you've held on longer than most would have. I'm almost impressed. Almost." He laughed again. "I just hope you stick around long enough to see what's coming."

On a raspy breath, Lucian took the bait. "What would that be?"

The leader of the Jackal clan walked around to face his enemy. "Well, I was going to make it a surprise, but I guess I'll tell you now. At this very moment, a hunting party is out looking for your sons. My soldiers have been instructed to either bring them to me in chains or bring me their heads"—he clasped his paws together and rubbed—"The anticipation is killing me. How do you feel about it? Are you as excited as I am to find out which it will be?" He paced in small circles before the strung-up coffin. "Of course, I'm hoping it will be in chains. I can't wait to see if they hold up to torture as well as you have."

Lucian pooled the saliva in his mouth and spat at the sadistic leader, hitting him squarely in his beady left eye. "Your soldiers will surely fail, and then I'll have something to celebrate, won't I?" he taunted.

The Jackal guard grabbed hold of the cage and violently shook it. "You'll pay for disrespecting Gortock," he growled.

Gortock wiped the spittle away and scowled at Lucian. "Bring the boiling water and give him a good dipping," he seethed through gritted teeth. "Let's see you celebrate that."

"With pleasure," the guard said with a merciless smile.

After they were out of sight, tears rolled down Lucian's cheek. If Damian and Logan didn't reach him soon, he would surely be dead, but his tears were for them. He didn't want to imagine the horrific things Gortock would do to them if they were captured.

TWENTY-FOUR

Mikael looked down at his feeble hands, slowly shook his head, and admitted, "Alas, I'm too old to be of any use, but I'll have first-aid supplies, as much as I can anyway, ready for the wounded's return. I imagine I'll need to have a couple of graves dug too."

"Well, maybe it won't come to that," Damian sighed. "But, we must be prepared for anything. Now, we must proceed with our attack before they make it to the village, or there will be more than a couple of graves needed." He looked to the others and waved his arm forward. "Let's advance but do it quietly. We need to have the element of surprise in our favor."

Tomas, Jon, and a scrawny man named Victor were the only villagers to join Damian and the others for the battle. The rest of the men stayed behind to guard the village, just in case they failed on their mission. The women had begged Valen to remain behind as well, but their cries were ignored by the wood nymph. She even insisted on being in front of the group with Damian, Logan, Dar, and Rutger.

"I might be more useful than you imagine. Remember, I can call upon the magic of the woods," she'd said with her chin defiantly jutted forth.

Logan scoffed at her, "I don't think making big flowers is going to help us, dear."

"I stopped you, didn't I?" she reminded him with a smirk.

"Shh," Damian hissed at them. "Do what you can," he told her while shooting a warning glance at Logan to mute him. "But don't be cocky."

"Do you think they know we're coming? I mean, can they smell us?" she whispered.

"I'm not sure, but I don't think their sense of smell is extraordinary. Their fighting skills are, though, so make sure you're alert."

She rolled her violet eyes as if to say his last remark was obvious. Then she stared at the sparse line of trees ahead of them and squinted. Out of nowhere, trees sprouted upward from the earth at an alarming rate.

"Stupid wench! You just told them we're here," Logan reprimanded.

Damian shot him a warning look to hush him from ranting further, though. "It's fine," he whispered, "Just draw your weapons. Hopefully, it slows them down, and they may not have even noticed."

Logan growled his disapproval but said nothing further. The other men already had their weapons in hand and were ready to take on whatever lay ahead. A rustling sounded nearby then grabbed the attention of all, but it was just a jackrabbit running from its den. With a sigh, the party continued forward and reached the hilltop. They hid within the thickened trees and peered down into the valley below. Movement among the shrubbery announced the presence of their enemy, and they lunged forward to make their first strike with their yells filling the hazy air.

The element of surprise was clearly there, as eleven pairs of widened eyes on growling faces stared back. Damian recalled that Logan had said that he'd counted at least fifteen of the creatures, which meant four more were hidden somewhere, and the eleven beasts they faced now wasted no time in making a counter-attack.

Damian and Logan both lunged for the three jackals in the front of the posse, while Dar and Rutger charged the flanks. The others in their small army advanced slowly to allow the immortals time to wound the beasts.

Valen remained alert and off to the side while the sound of steel clinking against steel and grunts filled the air. She, too, knew there were others hidden, and she sought them out with her keen vision. She quickly spied one in a treetop, who looked ready to pounce on Damian, so she blocked his maneuver with one of her own. She telepathically summoned the tree to entwine the Jackal with its vines. The creature yelped and struggled but to no avail. With his arms pinned, the warrior couldn't reach to cut himself free.

"Hmm, that's an interesting trick. Maybe I'll let you show me how to do that before I kill you," someone hissed in her ear as she felt something cold and sharp pressed into the small of her back. "Drop your dagger," the soldier commanded and then spun her around, so they were face to face.

Valen scowled at the stench of the warrior's breath and the sight of saliva dripping from his fangs. She met his appraising stare with a glare that would make a weaker soldier back down.

"Well, now, you're almost too pretty to kill, aren't you?" he snarled. "But, sadly, I'm not in a generous mood today." He flicked his wrist to plunge the dagger into her soft abdomen, oblivious that his hesitation gave some nearby dandelions time to weave their way around his ankles. Just as soon as the tip of the weapon pierced her flesh, he was yanked to the ground by the weeds. "What?" he cried out in confusion, and it was the last thing he would ever say. Damian had approached from behind and severed the warrior's head with his sword.

"Here"—he tossed Valen his canteen— "put some on your wound." She unscrewed the lid and put just two drops on the puncture and watched in relief as it closed. Then she screwed the lid on and tossed it back to him as three vicious warriors approached. "Get ready," he warned.

While Damian faced the bigger one, she braced herself for the other two. She sprang into the air, caught a vine distended from the closest tree, swung toward the warriors, and delivered a kick to both their heads. They stumbled backward just as she dropped to the ground behind them, daggers drawn, and plunged her steel blades into their backs. Their arms flailed in the air until they crumpled to their knees. She pulled the daggers out, cringing at the sensation of flesh slipping off the blades, and then plunged them into their necks. She spun around to see how Damian had fared and found him still in battle with the bigger soldier. She knew he'd be okay, though, so she ran to Oliver's side because he was under attack, and it looked like he was losing.

"Ah!" the small man shouted as he doubled over with his arms across his abdomen to keep his insides from spilling out. It was obvious that the wound inflicted was mortal.

Valen leapt onto the warrior's back and sliced her dagger across this throat. When he fell forward, with her still clinging to his muscular shoulders, she plunged her other knife into his back. Damian had come up behind them, and he quickly doused Oliver's stomach with some of the spring water. The wound closed, and the man scrambled to his feet. He clasped Damian's arm with a grateful squeeze.

"I know that I refused to drink the magical water before, but I'm ever so grateful that you have it now," he gushed. "I wasn't prepared to join my Hilda just yet."

"Don't celebrate until this is over," Damian warned before running off to help Victor. He was too late this time, though. The man's head lay next to his body by the time Damian got to his side. He knew that the spring water wouldn't be able to help this time, so he left the corpse and sought revenge.

The fighting lasted several more minutes, but when it was over, the Jackal hunting party was defeated. Sadly, though, Damian's group had lost two of its own—Tomas had joined Victor in death.

TWENTY-FIVE

After the dead were buried and prayers were said, they built a large bonfire and roasted a couple of hogs to celebrate what was otherwise a victory. Then, after they had enough to eat, the group packed up to continue the journey north to Budapest. When they reached the Tisza River, they stopped to set up camp for the night.

Damian, feeling protective of Valen even though she had proved her battle skills earlier in the day, made his bed next to her, and her soft breathing finally lulled him to sleep. He dreamed about being with her in the river again, but this time, it was just the two of them, and she was bathing him. His skin tingled from the soft touch of her delicate hands, and his state of arousal was painfully evident. Her hands worked a trail over his broad shoulders, down his muscled arms, and then over his chiseled torso. She lingered there, out of modesty, before moving on to his taut thighs. He watched the water crest over her dusky peaks while she washed him, and the urge to draw them into his mouth was almost too powerful to resist. His desire to possess her was a demon waging war inside him, and he desperately wanted to surrender.

Damian stirred on the hard ground, and his eyes flew open. He bolted upright and searched the darkness to get his bearings. A dream. It was just a dream.

Loud snoring filled the otherwise quiet night air, and he appeared to be the only one awake. He looked down at Valen's peaceful form and found himself wondering about her dreams. Was she dreaming about him too? He wanted to touch her, perhaps just a gentle stroke on her arm, but he didn't want to alarm her, so he refrained. He knew that the throbbing erection his dream had created would keep him awake, so he didn't even try to go back to sleep. Instead, he decided to go for a walk along the riverbank.

A few hundred feet away from the camp, he stumbled across a brown bear wading in the river, trying to catch his evening meal. He wasn't sure if it was the frustration brought on by the battle that day or the frustration brought on by his dream, but he lunged for the hungry animal, which had been too busy fishing to notice him. He struggled with the beast in the river current and received a few blows from its claws before he was successful in taking it down. Then, to his surprise, he sank his teeth into the bear's neck and ripped it open to feed. When he finished his meal, he threw the remaining carcass onto the bank for the scavengers to finish off. He looked at it for a couple of minutes before heading back to the campsite, though. The mark of the wolf lived again.

TWENTY-SIX

Damian never did fall back asleep. Instead, he watched over Valen and contemplated his stirring of feelings. He'd never let his heart grow fond of a woman before, so the sensation made him feel somewhat uncomfortable. Then, as he thought about the looming battle, he felt sorrowful. Maybe he could convince her to drink the water if he told her about his growing affection.

The sun had just risen, so it was time to wake everyone up—they still had a long journey ahead. Once everyone had roused, they shared a quick breakfast of dried meat and bread and then sharpened their weapons using large rocks found along the riverbank.

Jon approached Damian while everyone finished packing up. "I recommend traveling the rest of the way to the village Kiskörös. We might be able to find more men willing to fight with us."

Damian scratched his chin in thought. "Well, if we can do it quickly, then sure. The more help we have the better, but I don't want to delay our journey. We'll have to recruit and be immediately back on our way."

Jon nodded in agreement. "Sure, I understand. I was also thinking, though, that you may need to feed again."

Damian was surprised a human would offer him the opportunity to feed. He was also surprised that he didn't have the appetite to do so, especially since he'd been going without lately. It must be because of the stirring wolf.

"Are you ready to go, Brother?" Logan suddenly asked from behind him.

Damian spun around and explained the new plan to his twin.

"Good, we need the help, and then you can eat," Logan replied.

Damian shrugged his muscular shoulders. "I don't need to. I don't have the craving for human blood right now."

Logan squinted his eyes at his brother. "How is that? You always have the urge to feed. Is it because of the wood nymph?"

Damian looked off into the distance and softly replied, "No, I think it's because of the wolf. I feel its heart beating inside me again."

Logan's lips turned up into a big smile, and he howled. "I think that's amazing, and Father will be so pleased! It will be great to have a pack again."

Damian frowned at the mention of their father. "Not if we don't get to him in time, so let's be on our way." He signaled to the others, and they began the trek.

***

It was a couple of hours before they reached the relatively quiet village of Kiskörös. The inhabitants immediately had their guard up against the group of strangers, demanding why their travels had brought them to the village. Damian quickly explained to avoid a fight.

"Oh, well then that's okay," a man they called Jacob said. He seemed to be the one in command. "I'll even go with you. You'll find my fighting skills unmatched in these parts."

Damian assessed the man, but it was Logan who replied, "We shall see about that. Grab your weapons and anyone who will join us. Time is of the essence."

"Right away," Jacob said and dismissed himself. Several minutes later, he returned with Arthur, Brennan, and Cole, carrying an arsenal of weapons and a supply of food and water. Things were looking up.

"This is great. Thank you for joining us," Damian told them with a genuine smile.

Arthur answered for the group of men. "We are happy to help bring down Gortock and his army of jackals. They have tormented our peaceful existence for many years now."

"Aye, it's time they were driven far away from Hungary!" Cole exclaimed.

Logan growled, catching their attention. "We don't want to just drive them away; we want to slaughter every last one of them." The group cheered in agreement while raising their weapons in the air.

They kissed their families good-bye and disappeared from sight as they began the long journey. It would be two days before they reached Budapest.

TWENTY-SEVEN

The group of warriors traveled northwest to the Danube River and followed its winding path. The mortals fished for their supper, Valen ate some of the nearby vegetation, and the twins hunted in the forest. Damian matched Logan's skills in taking down large game. He also matched his brother's appetite for the animal flesh. He saw no reason to fight the call of the wolf. It was his birthright, after all, and he wouldn't ignore it. His mind flashed to Valen, and he considered the possibility that maybe she'd have him if he was no longer a vampire. She would surely be glad to know that the call of human blood wasn't as loud as it had been. He'd never wanted the curse bestowed upon him, and he would be glad to finally be rid of it.

Logan looked at him with a broad grin. "You're really taking to your heritage, and it's about damn time."

"It's not as if I ever had a say in the matter," Damian mumbled in between bites of the elk meat.

"I know that," Logan said and rolled his brown eyes. He looked up at the setting sun. "I think we should keep moving. We can light torches, but I can feel a full moon rising, which should light the way enough for us."

Damian looked at the cloudless sky too. "Aye, it might be enough to see by. I suppose we could always try it and then make camp if necessary. I'm in vote of getting to Father as soon as possible, but the others will need some sleep before they can battle. They aren't like us, you know?"

"Humph, it would be better if they were," Logan mumbled mostly to himself.

Damian began to laugh at an image flashing behind his eyes. His amusement received a look of annoyance from his brother, so he explained, "I don't think the world is ready for two of you."

Logan popped his neck and then his knuckles. "I think the world would be great if there were more of me"—he tilted his head sideways—"Maybe I should procreate."

"Hmm, a pack of Logans running around. That's just plain scary," Damian teased.

"Very funny. Let's get back to camp and make our way." The twins left the remaining meat for the woodland creatures and trotted back to the others.

"We're going to keep traveling," Damian announced to the attentive group. "We can use torches if you need them."

Valen stepped closer to him and proclaimed, "I have a better idea that won't announce our presence to any Jackal warriors who may be out hunting." Before he could ask what it was, she closed her eyes and held her palms out face-up.

A huge swarm of fireflies appeared and fluttered all around them, their lights flashing like beacons of hope and illuminating the darkening sky. Between the insects and the full moon, night travel would be feasible for them.

"Neat trick," Logan acknowledged with a grin, which was the closest he would ever get to stating his appreciation.

Valen nodded in response, but to Damian, she said, "I hope that will help."

He reached out and gently stroked her cheek. "It does help. You continue to amaze me with your gifts."

She shrugged her small shoulders and winked. "Well, I'm no wolf, but I have my uses."

Damian's brows furrowed. "You can tell?"

Her light laughter filled the air and caused the others to look their way. "I've been with you for several days now. I can tell there's been a shift."

He looked deep into her hypnotic purple eyes and wet his lips. "How do you feel about that?"

Her mouth slowly pulled up in one corner. "I think it's a good thing."

Damian wasn't used to blushing, but he felt one coming on. He even broke their eye contact, looking down at his meaty hands. "I'm glad," he replied and then turned away from her. He wasn't ready for that kind of conversation. He needed to free his father first and then dive into his feelings...if she survived.

TWENTY-EIGHT

The night journey north was incident-free except for a stumble on the loose river rock now and then. When it was apparent that the mortals were too tired to continue, Damian called for them to halt and make camp for the remainder of the night. Again, he slept protectively next to Valen, and again, lustful dreams plagued him. He woke up thinking that he would need to act upon them soon or go mad. He wouldn't force his will upon her, though, and he wasn't used to slow seduction. He watched her sleep out of the corner of his eye, afraid that if he stared directly at her, he would ravish her body on the spot. He decided to go for a walk again.

Damian was a quarter-mile away from the others when he heard the snapping of twigs behind him. He turned, expecting to find prey or Logan, but he found Valen instead.

"What are you doing all the way out here?" she asked quietly even though no one was around to hear her.

"I couldn't sleep, so I decided to go hunting," he replied while looking down. He was afraid if he looked into her eyes, she'd know he was lying.

"Oh, well, would you like some company? I could walk with you," she offered with a hopeful note in her voice.

He looked at her this time. "I would enjoy your company very much." Without thinking about it, he reached out and took her small hand in his.

Valen looked up in surprise, but she was wearing a satisfied smile, so it boosted his confidence. He gave her hand a gentle squeeze and led her toward a clearing. He could smell rabbits nearby, but he wasn't thinking about food. Instead, he was thinking that it might be now or never if he wanted to be with her as her lover. They'd soon be in Budapest, and it was a real possibility that something awful could happen to her.

When they stepped into the meadow, the wildflowers responded to her presence by swaying in her direction. They seemed to move with every step she took. Damian bent down and swiftly picked a few for her as a romantic gesture.

"Here you go," he mumbled shyly and handed them to her.

Her eyes widened at his thoughtfulness, and a big smile graced her small mouth. "Thank you"—she pulled them to her nose and inhaled their fragrance—"They're lovely and smell delicious." She took a small nibble of one, and then laughed when he grimaced.

"I don't understand how you can eat that stuff," he murmured.

"Back at you," she replied with another giggle.

He shrugged but with a grin. "Fair enough I suppose. To each his own, right?"

She bobbed her head, and her tendrils bounced over her shoulder to spill down toward her bosom, captivating his gaze. Before he could stop himself, he leaned in and gently pressed his lips to hers. When she didn't resist his advance, he parted her lips with his tongue and plundered her warm mouth. He didn't even care that he could taste the flower she'd been munching on. Their tongues danced in an erotic tango while his hands gripped her waist, and with every stroke of his lips against hers, his need grew more intense. He broke the kiss to look at her, and his finger traced the delicate softness of her swollen lips. His other hand gently squeezed her hip and then traveled to her small, round bottom as he pulled her into his body, so she could feel his desire pressed against her. He could feel her trembling as he leaned in to softly nuzzle her neck. He hoped it was from excitement and not fear—it suddenly occurred to him that she might be a virgin, and that was unfamiliar territory for him. He didn't want to hurt her, so he removed his hands and lips and stepped backward. She looked surprised at his response, and her mouth turned down in a pout.

"What's wrong?" Her question filled the sudden silence. "Don't you want me?"

Damian tilted his head and studied her features, which had a gossamer glow in the moonlight, and he decided he couldn't allow himself to taint her purity. "Of course, I want you. I've wanted you ever since that day in the river, if not before then, but I don't want to hurt you."

Valen approached him with small steps. "I'm not worried about you hurting me. I'm worried about dying without ever feeling your touch. I want to know what it's like between a man and a woman. I want to know what it's like with you." She reached up and lightly played her fingertips on his cheek. "Will you show me?"

A storm of emotion whirled inside him as he studied her eyes. He could tell she was serious, and that should've eased his mind, yet he still felt troubled. It would be too easy to take her into his arms and show her what passion was. It would be too easy to succumb to the beast howling inside him for her. Now or never. The warning rang through his mind again. It was all he needed to hear.

"If you insist," he replied in a sultry growl as he leaned in to claim her mouth again. His hands roamed her petite form with a fervor he couldn't hide. He unbelted her shift and pushed it up to where he could cup her perky breasts while his tongue continued to play with hers. He roamed his thumbs over her firm nipples while massaging her small mounds. She broke the kiss off long enough to remove her garment in a quick fluid motion while his greedy stare seared her flesh.

"Am I the only one going to undress?" she asked with amusement dancing in her voice.

A throaty growl escaped him before he yanked his clothing off. It was her turn to stare now, and it spurred his lust. He scooped her into his arms, with her head tucked under his chin, and carried her to a soft patch of grass where he lay her down. He carefully lowered himself over her and drew her taut peak into his hungry mouth to suckle. The soft mewing sounds of pleasure she made caused the throbbing between his muscular thighs to intensify, and he felt crazed. His hand reached for her mound of soft downy curls, but then it hesitated. He had to go slow with her to make her body ready for him. He softly pressed his hand to the damp curls that gathered around her cleft. She might be a wood nymph, but she still had the body of a woman. Slowly, he pressed a finger between her folds and let it slip the length of her softness. She grabbed a fistful of his hair in response and let out a high-pitched cry.

"Am I hurting you in any way?" he asked, his voice saturated with concern.

"No. Please continue what you're doing," she responded on a pant and then writhed against his hand, losing herself to the sensation.

He continued working her delicate flesh until he could deny himself her molten heat no further. He rose over her, pressed himself to her moist opening, and slowly impaled her. As he felt himself pushing past her maidenhead, he held his breath in anticipation of her pain. She was a true warrior, though. She let out a soft whimper and dug her fingers into the flesh of his chest and shoulder. At first, she lay still while he stroked her insides, but then she began to move in rhythm with him. Her eager movements to ride his shaft quickly brought him to release, but it felt empty without having given her one of her own.

He apologized, "I'm sorry that it wasn't pleasurable for you too." Then he slowly withdrew from her body.

She was still panting from the experience, but she reached up to stroke his cheek again and whispered, "I liked it. I liked the feeling of you inside me."

"But it hurt you," he murmured against her neck before planting a gentle kiss.

She surprised him with a soft laugh. "I was stabbed in battle today, and I can assure you that hurt worse. Besides, doesn't it get better the next time?"

He smiled down at her while running his fingers through her silky hair. "I promise you it gets better." He pulled her into his body, with her form molding perfectly against his, and they fell asleep together with fireflies dancing all around.

TWENTY-NINE

A splash of sunlight on his face woke Damian from a deep sleep. He smiled when he remembered it was Valen snuggled against him, and he instinctively wrapped his arm tighter around her. She stirred, and her eyes fluttered open.

"Good morning," he greeted her as her violet eyes focused on him.

With a soft smile, she replied, "Good morning."

"How do you feel? Are you okay?"

A blush crept into her cheeks. "I'm a little sore, but I feel great. I feel different."

He cocked a brow at her. "Different in a good way?"

"Yes, I think so"—she briefly looked away, and the blush returned—"But I think we should do that again, so I can be certain."

Damian's smile broadened. "Well, if you insist," he teased playfully and ran his fingertip down her naked body.

"I do insist." She leaned closer to his mouth and wet her lips before planting a passionate kiss on him.

He accepted the caress of her mouth with a voracious hunger, and his already pulsing manhood reached its maximum size. Valen broke the kiss off and thrust her breasts toward his lips.

"Please put your mouth on them again," she begged.

He hungrily suckled both blushing peaks while his hands cupped her buttocks, giving them a firm squeeze. She moaned from delight, and just the sound of it made him come close to bursting.

"I need you now," he growled and lifted her above him. He gently and slowly impaled her on his thick shaft while watching her eyes close and her mouth form a perfect O. She winced a little at first, but then her face relaxed, as did her body, as she accepted the full size of him.

She began to ride him with slow, tentative movements, but then, as her body grew accustomed to the sensation of him, her tempo increased. He watched her breasts bounce with her body and reached out to play with them. He lightly pinched her tips this time while watching her expression to make sure it was one of pleasure. She seemed to be enjoying the love making this time, and that made his heart flutter.

"Here," he said with a sultry growl, "try this." He cupped her buttocks again, lifted her up slightly, and then pumped his hips with increasing speed.

Her expression tightened along with her fleshy walls as he brought her closer to release. When it was upon her, her eyes rolled back, and she cried out his name. This brought his own climax to fruition, and he grunted in ecstasy while his seed filled her body. After the shuddering stopped, he gently lifted her off and placed her next him. He nuzzled the top of her head while tracing his fingertips along her arm. The softness of her skin amazed him.

"You know, we really need to go back to camp. I'm sure the others are awake and eager to continue our travels," he mentioned with disappointment.

"I'm sure you're correct," she replied, and her tone was just as sorrowful.

With heavy hearts, they dressed and walked back to the encampment to meet several questioning stares.

Logan, naturally, didn't let it slide. "What do we have here? Where were you all night?"

Damian glared at his twin. He didn't want Valen to be embarrassed in front of everyone, so he responded, "We scouted out the area to make sure there weren't any more hunting parties nearby."

Logan's lip curled into a smug grin. "Sure. If you say so."

"Anyway, let's get going. We should be able to reach Budapest today," Damian mumbled while gathering his pack. He fingered the canteen, which still held a couple of drops of spring water, and turned to Valen.

"Will you please reconsider?" he asked while holding the container out.

She hesitated before she replied, "I told you how I feel about that."

His heart fell, and he felt cut off from air. "I know what you said, but then last night... I just thought it changed things." She looked deep into his searching eyes, and he heard her swallow. "I want things to change in my life. I'm tired of being alone, and you are like no other woman. I know that if something happens to you, I won't be able to live with myself. I have to protect you, and this is the best way."

She tilted her head and sighed. "You're speaking like I'm going to die, but I don't intend to."

He couldn't stop from grinning at her self-assurance. "Okay, well, let's say you come out of the battle just fine then. I'm not going to age. I will never get sick or die. I'll have to say good-bye to you eventually, and I don't want to."

She looked down at her small hands, which she wrung nervously. "Well, I still have time to think about it. For now, let's just be on our way and enjoy the time we do have together."

Damian nodded with a frown and then assembled the group. "We should be in Budapest in just a few hours. When we get closer, a few of us will travel ahead to search for points of attack and any hunting parties."

"Good idea, Brother," Logan exclaimed. "Now let's get walking."

Everyone's nerves were on edge as they began the last part of the trek to what could be their demise. Even the immortals were filled with concern—lives would certainly be lost, and they wouldn't all belong to the Jackal clan.

THIRTY

The small group of warriors was closing in on Budapest, so it was time for the scouting party to go forth. It was composed of Damian, Logan, Rutger, and Jon. The others quietly made camp, with guards on duty, and were instructed not to burn any fires because the smoke would alert the Jackals.

Damian squeezed Valen's hand and whispered to her, "I'll be back soon. Be on the alert."

She nodded slowly and gave him a kiss on the lips, not caring if the others saw.

"Not now, Brother," Logan moaned. "There will be time for that later."

Damian ignored him and stared into Valen's mysterious eyes. He assured her, "He's right. There will be time."

She mouthed, "Hurry back," before gathering with the others who were staying behind.

Damian watched her while walking away. She was picking up a sword and putting herself on duty as one of the guards. If only she'd drink the magical water.

"It'll be all right," Logan suddenly said with sincerity. "She's a good warrior. She'll hold her own."

Damian mumbled back, "Aye, she is. I just hope that'll be enough because she still refuses the water."

Logan glanced sideways at him. "Do you want to spend eternity with her? I never thought you to be that kind of man."

Damian didn't need any time to consider his response. He quickly replied, "Aye, I do, Brother. She's gotten inside me."

Logan looked up at the sky with a silly grin, causing Damian to quirk a brow at him. "What are you doing?"

"I'm just looking for flying pigs. I never expected you to fall in love," Logan teased and lightly punched him in the shoulder. Damian quickly grabbed him and put him in a headlock while the others watched and laughed. "Okay, okay," Logan said with a strangled laugh, "I give."

"Enough horseplay," Damian warned in a hushed voice and let go of his twin. "I think I heard something coming this way."

***

Back at the makeshift camp, Valen paced nervously along with Liam, Jacob, and Cole, watching the forest for any sign of movement. A deer startled them when it quickly darted by, but other than that, it was quiet.

Valen glanced over at Damian's pack and the canteen dangling from it. She wanted to live longer if only to be in his naked embrace again. Taking care of the forest was her only purpose in life, but Damian was giving her a new one. She wanted to be with him wherever he went when the battle was over, even if it took her away from the woods and everything she knew. Never in her existence, did she imagine she'd fall in love or experience the physical pleasures a woman felt with a human man, which completely broke the rules of her breed. Wood nymphs weren't supposed to interact with humans, much less fall in love with one. They were born of special flowers and woodland magic, which they would then spend their lives protecting, and she was clearly stepping away from that destiny. She would give it all up, though, if she could spend her life in his embrace, and she didn't care if anyone blamed her.

A sudden rustling among the trees made her spin around. A Jackal soldier lunged at her, but she was light on her feet and able to dodge him. Unfortunately, though, he wasn't alone and two others were soon upon her, tackling her to the ground. Liam and Cole rushed to her side while Jacob and others were defending the camp against another warrior, who came from the south.

Valen took a stab to her shoulder before Cole flung one jackal off her. She ignored the burning pain and jumped to her feet while slashing out at the other two jackals, who were frothing at the mouth from rage. She heard a high-pitched screech as soon as her sword sliced into one warrior's torso, but the second creature dodged the thrust of her dagger, and he backhanded her, sending her flying. She tried to scramble away when she saw him raise his sword, but she didn't have time, and the steel blade came crashing toward her. She quickly rolled, though, at the same time a shot rang out. The jackal fell forward and landed just a few inches away from her. She thrust her dagger into his neck before he could recover from the shot, and a crimson river spilled forth. She removed her weapon and sprang to her feet. The other Jackal soldiers had been killed, though, so she relaxed her stance and took a deep but painful breath. She became very aware of the fire in her shoulder.

I could've been killed and never felt his lips or touch again. Her eyes flashed to the canteen one more time while she sponged at the wound with a torn piece of her tunic.

***

Damian and the others were on high alert as they drew closer to Gortock's castle. The rustling among the trees had been two soldiers, whom they quickly and easily dispatched. They searched the outer wall of the fortress for the best points of entry, noting spots in the wall that looked weak. Then they stealthily checked out the main gate.

Damian nudged Logan and told him, "I think Dar and his group can use a log to ram the wall while you and I take a couple of others to the gate, which will be heavily guarded."

Logan quickly considered his idea and nodded. "Aye, or we could just all go through the wall."

"I think it's best if we split the soldiers' focus up, though, by spreading out," Damian argued.

"You're probably right," Logan relented. "Let's go get the others and attack."

They made haste back to the camp and found the others quietly waiting. As soon as Damian saw the dead soldiers, he scanned the group for Valen with panic gripping him by the throat. She was softly walking toward him with a sly smile playing on her pink lips. Without a word, she stood on her tiptoes, wrapped her arms around his neck, and gave him a deep, meaningful kiss.

"I'm so happy to see that you're okay," he told her with his voice full of emotion.

"I'm just fine," she whispered back. "Now, let's go get your father."

THIRTY-ONE

The twelve new friends crept quietly toward the castle in the early evening hours. They knew it was going to be difficult to seize the fortress, since they were few in number, so a surprise attack was their best chance. Damian and Logan did most of the planning, but the others were okay with letting them lead.

The first wave was fire. They lit several torches and threw them over the castle wall, hoping the blaze would distract the jackals long enough to ram it down, and the plan seemed to be working as sounds of mayhem filled the air. However, they failed to notice a couple of soldiers who had climbed to the top of the wall while they were ramming it, and arrows were soon raining down on them. Jacob took one in the chest and crumpled to the earth while the others ducked for cover.

Damian quickly picked up one of the arrows and chucked it as hard as he could at an archer. It plunged into the soldier's throat, and he fell from the wall. Logan sprang up the barrier like a lithe cat and grabbed the other shooter by his ankle, yanking him from his perch while thrusting his dagger into the creature's stomach. Logan then climbed the rest of the way over and jumped down on top of unsuspecting soldiers who were still battling the blazing grass. Damian heard his brother snarl and knew that he had either transformed into the beast, or he was at least half-way there.

The wall gave in and crumbled down around them, giving them an eyeful of the chaos ahead. Several soldiers ran in their direction, while others were still trying to put out the fires. Then there was the startling sight of a huge werewolf battling three soldiers. Logan hadn't removed his clothing, so they hung from his body in shreds. Damian watched his twin as he ripped out the throat of one jackal with his teeth while simultaneously raking his immense claws across the abdomen of another. The third had jumped onto his massive back and stabbed him, but he flung him off, while the wound healed itself, and then crashed on top of him with his sword buried into the soldier's body.

Damian and the others were already deep in battle with the army that had flooded upon them when Logan finished with the trio of jackals. He rushed to their side, and ripped into each one he could get his paws on. When the numbers had dwindled, he shifted back into human form.

"Let's find Father," he growled to Damian while fighting off another soldier.

Damian shot a look over his soldier at Valen, who had been fiercely holding her own. She met his gaze and called out, "Find your father. I'm okay." Then he watched in horror as she was drawn through with a sword.

The world seemed to stop spinning as he watched the bloody weapon being removed from her body by Oliver, who'd already decapitated the responsible jackal. Damian found his strength to move and rushed to her side while she was still bent over, gripping her stomach. He grabbed the canteen, which was fastened to his waste, and opened the lid to drip the water onto her gaping wound. When he turned the canister over, though, nothing trickled out. Helplessness burned in every cell of his body as he realized she would die in his arms, and there was nothing he could do to stop it—Logan wasn't around with the other canteen.

Damian didn't even notice the jackal that was leaping toward him with his dagger in hand, so he took a massive blow in between his shoulders. Brokenhearted, he fell to his knees and wished he could die. The Jackal soldier charged him again with a sword aimed at his throat, but he didn't care. He watched, unmoving, as the sword was raised into the air for a violent swing, and he braced himself for the blow that would offer him sweet release. A blur suddenly shot by, though, and the warrior was taken down before he could attack. Damian was stunned as he recognized the green tunic his savior was wearing. He didn't understand how, but it was Valen. She was alive and incredibly spry as she tackled and killed the soldier. When she turned to face Damian, she looked perfectly fine and was wearing a big smile.

He stared at her with his mouth gaping. "I don't understand. How are you…did you…how?" he stammered.

Still smiling, she told him, "I took your advice."

He followed her gaze, which had settled on the empty canteen. "Do you mean?" He looked back at her with a huge smile.

"Yes, but let's discuss that later. We have your father to save."

Damian looked around with a lightened heart. Logan had already run off in search of their father, and it was indeed time to catch up. His brother was capable of fierce battle, but who knew how many soldiers remained. Hand in hand, they ran around the western side of the castle to the backside, slaying every Jackal warrior they came across. The others had stayed behind to finish fighting the first swarm.

When they reached their destination, the view terrified Damian yet again. He saw his frail father hanging from the gables, imprisoned inside a torture coffin. He could see the oozing wounds inflicted in the king's back and the iron kettle encasing the lower region of his prison. It had a fire blazing below it.

"For God's sake, they're boiling him!" he shouted and ran toward the small battalion Logan was battling.

While he ran, with Valen keeping pace at his side, rage singed his veins. He felt his muscles stretching to the limit and his bones cracking. He felt as if he was being pulled apart, and it burned like hell's inferno. He stopped short of the weapon-wielding throng of soldiers and succumbed to the pain. He knew what was happening—he was shifting into the werewolf. He just didn't know that it would hurt so much. He stared at his hands as his fingers elongated and claws painfully grew where his nails had been. The pain in his jaw, as it too elongated and sprouted longer, sharper fangs, was almost unbearable. He rode it out, though, until the shift was complete. He'd grown incredibly larger and felt twice as strong as he had in vampire form. Now, the only burning he felt was his fury.

Valen was already fighting alongside Logan, who was clearly relieved to see her. Damian joined them in just a few long sprints. He ran faster than ever before with his newfound stamina. Logan looked up, after removing the head of a jackal, and smiled. Then he shifted too.

While fighting the soldiers, Damian made eye contact with his dying father and saw something in his eyes that he'd not seen in what seemed like forever. On top of the evident relief, he saw pride. His father finally had his wolf family back. Lucian used what little stamina he had left to give a nod to his firstborn son while Valen used her new strength to move the scalding kettle away from him.

Dar, Rutger, Arthur, Liam, and Brennan showed up then and helped with the fight. Limbs and blood spewed everywhere as the jackals were defeated one by one. After the soldiers were all dispatched, the ground was littered with corpses. Unfortunately, Arthur and Liam were among the dead, but they had made a great sacrifice and had fought well. Logan changed back and grabbed Damian's arm.

"Damian, I'm going after Gortock. He must be hiding in the castle. You get Father out and give him this"—he threw his canteen to Damian— "Then, come find me."

Damian nodded in his twin's direction while he raced to Valen's side. He used his dagger to pry the lock open and yanked the cage apart, catching his father's body as it crumpled forward. The once strong king felt limp like wet noodles in his son's arms. Damian cradled him to his chest while Valen unscrewed the lid on the canteen of mystical water.

Lucian's eyes fluttered as he took in the sight of his son and the mysterious woman. He saw a familiar look exchange between them—he saw his son's face grow incredibly soft when he looked at the pretty woman, and he recognized it as adoration.

In a weak voice, he stated, "You've found love."

Tears streamed from Damian's eyes as he poured some of the water over his father's legs—what was left of them. His flesh had been boiled down to the bone, and infection had settled in. Then he brought the nozzle to his father's mouth.

"Aye, I've found love, Father, and I've found the Sacred Spring. Drink this and you will be stronger than you ever were. Your kingdom will live again."

He expected Lucian to accept the water, but his father shook his head. "No, my son. My time is done here. It's time for me to join your mother, and it's time for you and Logan to reign over Drago"—his gaze settled on Valen—"She'll be your queen."

Fear clouded Damian's dark eyes, and his body began to tremble. He couldn't believe that his father was giving up, but then he recalled earlier when he'd been ready to do the same because he thought Valen was dead. Still, he couldn't let his father die.

"Father, please, you don't know what you're saying. You're going to be fine, and we'll all rule Drago if that's what you wish. We'll rule as a clan of wolves again."

Lucian's eyes closed briefly, but then he mumbled, "No, I don't want to live without your mother. My son, you've been in search of yourself ever since the vampires changed you. Now, somehow, you've reidentified with your birthright, and I couldn't be more pleased. I can die in peace, knowing that you and your brother are safe and that you are loved. Enjoy each other." A final sigh escaped his lips, and he closed his eyes for the last time.

Damian continued to hold him while sobbing over his limp body. He didn't even look up at Valen when she placed a gentle hand on his shoulder. He did look up, though, when a heavy door swung open and Logan appeared with Gortock flung over his shoulder in a vice-like grip.

Logan saw his brother's tears and instinctively knew that their father had passed. He threw Gortock to the ground with a fierce growl and tossed his head back with a loud howl. Damian grabbed the leader as he tried to scramble away, even though some of his bones had broken on impact with the ground. Valen took Lucian's body into her own embrace as Damian stood, still holding Gortock's ankle. He grabbed the leader's left wrist while Logan grabbed the wrist and ankle on the other side. Then they carried him to the burning fire and lowered his screaming body into it just far enough that his back was lit ablaze. With a nod from Damian, Logan began to back away, and Damian did the same. A loud cracking and tearing sound pierced the air with horrific screams as the jackal's body was quartered. Without flinching, the brothers picked up the limbs and torso and threw them into the flame.

"Why wouldn't he drink the water?" Logan asked when he saw the open canteen.

Damian looked down and slowly shook his head. "He said he wanted to be with Mother, and it was our time to rule Drago. I couldn't convince him to change his mind."

Logan snorted a laugh. "Sounds like him. He has always been stubborn." Then he nodded in Valen's direction. "And her?"

Damian finally met the wood nymph's stare. "She'll be coming with us," he stated matter-of-factly.

"All right then. Let's get going," Logan said with a slight grin. He took their father's body from Valen, so they could find a spot to bury him.

"What about us?" Dar asked on behalf of himself, Oliver, and Rutger. "The men from Kiskörös are on their way back home, but we don't really have anything to go back to."

Damian looked at his twin and then back to Dar. "Well, we need soldiers if we are going to rebuild the kingdom of Drago. How would you feel about joining us there?"

Dar looked at his companions, who nodded in agreement. "Aye. We'll go with you."

Damian turned to Valen and stroked her arm with his fingertips. "And I need a queen. Are you up for it?"

A blush hit her cheeks, but she answered with her chin jutted forth, "I'll be everything you want me to be."

"Let's go home then, my queen," he said with a grin and proffered his arm to her.

The men carried the bodies of Lucian, Liam, and Arthur to a pretty meadow and buried them, using a shovel they'd found in Gortock's castle. They said a prayer, and then Valen touched the ground, causing beautiful flowers to instantly cover the fresh graves.

The twins shared a knowing glance as they stood over their father's final resting spot. It would be difficult to get over the deaths of their mother

and father, but they still had much to look forward
to as they rebuilt the kingdom of Drago.